"Watch out!"

Clive's jaw clinched as he went around a sharp curve at too fast of a speed while pulling the trailer. The trailer slid off onto the gravel and fishtailed before he got it back onto the pavement.

Holly's heart hitched in her chest. The SUV sped up beside them. "Can you not go faster?"

"Won't do any good. We can't possibly outrun them pulling the trailer." Clive's jaw twitched, like he was considering the situation.

The SUV swung and hit the back end of Clive's trailer, sending it fishtailing again. This time his truck went halfway off the road. A steep ditch lined the road.

She shrieked. "Oh no."

Clive left off the accelerator as he held onto the steering wheel.

A small car came from the other direction. Holly desperately wanted Clive to do something, but she didn't know what he could do while pulling the trailer. Again, the SUV started to come around him, and Clive hit the brakes.

It was too late. The SUV plowed into the side of his trailer...

Connie Queen has spent her life in Texas, where she met and married her high school sweetheart. Together they've raised eight children and are enjoying their grandchildren. Today, as an empty nester, Connie lives with her husband and her Great Dane, Nash, and is working on her next suspense novel.

Books by Connie Queen

Love Inspired Suspense

Justice Undercover
Texas Christmas Revenge
Canyon Survival
Abduction Cold Case
Tracking the Tiny Target
Rescuing the Stolen Child
Wilderness Witness Survival
Searching for Justice

Thunder Ridge Justice

Shielded by the Cowboy

Visit the Author Profile page at LoveInspired.com.

SHIELDED BY THE COWBOY

CONNIE QUEEN

LOVE INSPIRED SUSPENSE
INSPIRATIONAL ROMANCE

If you purchased this book without a cover you should be aware that this book is stolen property. It was reported as "unsold and destroyed" to the publisher, and neither the author nor the publisher has received any payment for this "stripped book."

MIX
Paper | Supporting responsible forestry
FSC® C021394

LOVE INSPIRED® SUSPENSE
INSPIRATIONAL ROMANCE

Recycling programs for this product may not exist in your area.

ISBN-13: 978-1-335-95749-8

Shielded by the Cowboy

Copyright © 2025 by Connie Queen

All rights reserved. No part of this book may be used or reproduced in any manner whatsoever without written permission.

Without limiting the exclusive rights of any author, contributor or the publisher of this publication, any unauthorized use of this publication to train generative artificial intelligence (AI) technologies is expressly prohibited. Harlequin also exercises their rights under Article 4(3) of the Digital Single Market Directive 2019/790 and expressly reserves this publication from the text and data mining exception.

This is a work of fiction. Names, characters, places and incidents are either the product of the author's imagination or are used fictitiously. Any resemblance to actual persons, living or dead, businesses, companies, events or locales is entirely coincidental.

For questions and comments about the quality of this book, please contact us at CustomerService@Harlequin.com.

® is a trademark of Harlequin Enterprises ULC.

Love Inspired
22 Adelaide St. West, 41st Floor
Toronto, Ontario M5H 4E3, Canada
www.LoveInspired.com

HarperCollins Publishers
Macken House, 39/40 Mayor Street Upper,
Dublin 1, D01 C9W8, Ireland
www.HarperCollins.com

Printed in Lithuania

What time I am afraid, I will trust in thee.
In God I will praise his word, in God I have put
my trust; I will not fear what flesh can do unto me.
—*Psalm* 56:3–4

I would like to dedicate this book to my dad, Tex Autry Monk. It's not that he would've ever read a romance book, but he would've asked me how it was going. He was a man with a sense of humor, normally sarcastic in nature. Along with my mom, he raised five kids, taking them to church, eating every meal together and taught us the importance of God and family.

He worked a variety of jobs to support us, from farming to owning his own auto repair business, and then back to ranching when he retired. By the time I published my first book, he was already gone, but sometimes I wonder what he would've had to say about it. I'm sure whatever he chose to say, it would've made me laugh.

Love you.

ONE

Please don't die on me. Please don't die.

Holly Myers gripped the steering wheel as her car chugged again. The morning sun shone through the dirty windshield, the glare making it almost impossible to see. She only had a few more miles, according to her phone's GPS, to get to the seller's house.

She needed to buy a new vehicle and hoped the guy would come down on the price. And more importantly, that it would actually run. Seventeen hundred and thirteen dollars didn't give her any wiggle room. She'd bought her current jalopy only five weeks ago, and it already had a bad head gasket, which meant it wasn't worth repairing.

As she rounded the corner, the sedan died again. She drew a deep breath. *Please, don't fail me now.* She threw the vehicle into Park and pumped the gas three times before turning the ignition. It roared to life for the fifth time since leaving the small town fifteen miles ago. She didn't know how much longer the vehicle would hang on. But she did not want this guy from the buy and sell marketplace to know she was desperate. If so, he wouldn't go down on the price.

And she was desperate.

A swift kick inside her belly reminded her, not only

was her well-being at stake but also the life of her unborn baby girl. Thirteen weeks and two days until her due date.

Holly landed a job at the Greasy Griddle Diner just yesterday in Cedar Hollow, Texas. How was she supposed to get to work on time every day without a vehicle? The home she could afford was two miles outside of town. It might be fine to walk or ride a bike to work, but in a few weeks, her pregnancy would make it a challenge. She was six months along and hadn't started showing until about four weeks ago. Now, it seemed like she was getting bigger by the day.

At the "T," she turned left. The house sat on the right, back off the road about fifty yards. It didn't look like that nice of a home, and she hoped she wasn't being irresponsible by shopping for a car way out in the country. She had asked the seller if he would meet her in town, but he said he just did not have the time. He could only do it if she would pay an extra hundred dollars. There simply was no way she could afford that.

Her vehicle again jerked and died. This time when she put it into Park and turned the ignition, the engine wouldn't turn over and steam lifted from under the hood. *Oh no.* It would be obvious she was desperate for another vehicle. If only there was someone in the area to assist her, but she knew no one. Except for her new boss, a lady in her forties who had a no-nonsense demeanor. She didn't think that was the way to start a good working relationship by begging for help.

After three more unsuccessful attempts to start the vehicle, she got out and left it beside the road. She grabbed her purse and, with her head held high, walked down the driveway toward the house. She'd been in dire situations before and had learned if you acted confidently that it tended to go a long way. Some of the best advice she had gotten was from a teacher who told her years ago to quit apologizing for everything. *Don't slouch. Don't hold your head like your chin is a cinder block. Look people in the eyes. You have nothing to be ashamed of, so act like it.*

Even though she still struggled to do that, she had attempted to incorporate the advice into her life. And to her surprise, it seemed people didn't talk down to her as much.

As she drew closer to the home, she noticed there were three vehicles. One was a black Suburban that looked new. It had nice rims and tinted windows. The other was an older model pickup, but it was clean and parked under a single bay shed. The third vehicle was the one she had called about—a faded blue Honda Civic coupe. It sat off to the side about twenty yards. Grass grew up around it, making her wonder if the car even ran.

She was glad when no dogs raced out to greet her. Ever since she was a small child and had been bitten, she was leery. Sometimes, people in the country had several of them. As she approached the house, the sound of angry voices carried to her. Holly couldn't discern the words, but it was obvious some guy was mad.

"I didn't tell...baby...promise. Please don't..." Sporadically, words could be made out.

Her steps faltered. Being that she'd witnessed plenty of fights growing up, she had no desire to interrupt whatever problem was happening inside the home. She skirted wide of the driveway and closer to the Honda. Again, there was yelling. Holly stopped when she was beside the car as a lady wearing flip-flops ran out of the house.

The woman shrieked. Holly took a step her way when

suddenly a man dressed in a button-down shirt and tie stepped out with a rifle. Holly halted in her tracks.

A loud crack split the air, making her jump. The woman fell to the ground with a growing large red circle on her back.

Holly stifled the scream that bubbled up in her throat as she dropped to the ground.

More yelling came from inside the home and then three more quickly fired shots. Two shooters? Holly's breath was sucked from her. What was happening?

The man dressed in the tie disappeared inside the home.

Holly glanced at the building to make certain the gunman hadn't returned, and seeing no one, she dashed to the fallen lady as fast as her condition would allow. Pretty black, curly hair blew in the breeze across the woman's shoulder. Blood ran down her back, but Holly tried not to look at the gaping wound as she felt for a pulse. Nothing. The men's voices sounded again, and Holly darted behind the shed.

A man from inside the house demanded, "Haul Sabrina back inside here beside her husband and get rid of the evidence."

They had killed the woman's husband, too? She peeked around the corner. The man with the tie never glanced her way as he strode across the yard.

Holly wanted to run, but she didn't want the man to see her. Her chest squeezed as she refused to breathe for fear he would hear her. Heartlessly, he yanked the lady by her feet and dragged her across the yard, her head bouncing with each bump, up the back steps and into the house.

There were few places to hide. Even if she could get to it, her sedan was useless. She turned to the faded Honda she was supposed to purchase. Making sure she stayed low as possible, she hurried to the vehicle and climbed in on the passenger side.

She sank to her knees on the floorboard, her belly brushing against the seat, and stuck her head up just enough to see out of the driver's-side window. An older, clean-shaven bald man wearing a black T-shirt and jeans moved into the backyard, away from the house.

Finally, the younger, sharp dressed man came out of the house and jogged across the yard. When he got to the older man, he stopped, and they both looked at the house expectantly.

Seconds ticked by like they were waiting for something. What were they doing? She had the feeling it wasn't good.

Boom!

The house exploded into flames. Popping and sizzling filled the air, and Holly bowed her head and closed her eyes for just a couple of seconds. Even within the protection of the compact car, the heat could be felt.

The men's voices carried to her. The older one said, "Let's get out of here before someone notices the flames."

She had to do something. They couldn't get away with this. She didn't know who they were or why they killed these people, but they could not get away with murder.

She peeked over the seat to see if she could see the license plate of their vehicle but could only make out the first three digits: 7HJ. The two men hurried to get in their SUV, but the older guy stopped and looked toward her sedan parked at the end of the drive. "Where did that car come from?"

"It wasn't here before." The twentysomething male looked around.

A glimpse over the seat showed the man's gaze landing on the Civic. Keys dangled in the ignition. She didn't even know if this thing ran.

The bald man headed her way. The sun reflected off something at his waist. A policeman's badge.

In a panic, she scrambled into the driver's seat and turned the key as her heart stuck in her chest. The car started but immediately died. "Come on. Come on," she pleaded.

The coupe started again on the second try just as the man reached her door and yanked it open. She threw the vehicle into gear and hit the gas as the man grabbed her arm. She screamed and tried to get out of his grip. He held fast as she kept the accelerator down and clung to the wheel. She jerked right. Pain from his fingers biting into her flesh made her cry out again.

Finally, the man fell, and she continued to drive the little vehicle across the pasture. The low fuel gauge dinged, and the orange light came on. She kept the speed up as fast as the Civic would go. Holly grabbed the door and slammed it shut.

A glance in her rearview mirror showed the SUV was in hot pursuit. It was at least fifty yards behind her, but considering the coupe had less than an eighth of a tank of gas, it wouldn't be long before they caught her. She had to get away.

A row of trees showed up on her right, forcing her to go to the left. The car bounced up and down on the rough ground. Several times it bottomed out. The jarring made Holly even more tense.

"Don't stop. Come on, Holly, you've got this." She cringed as she gave herself the pep talk. There was a barbed wire fence on the other side of the trees, and a shallow ditch separated the pasture from a red dirt road. She kept the accelerator down and smashed into the fence. Screeching filled the air as the wire hit the front of the car. A couple of the strands went up and over her vehicle, but some of it was still attached. As she got on the road, she turned west. She didn't know where she was. Only that she had to get away. No doubt they would kill her for witnessing the murders.

At last, the barbed wire strands were either beneath her vehicle or had come loose. Dust filled the sky as the car sped down the country road. The dirt cloud was so huge she couldn't see if the SUV was behind her.

After another mile, the road came to a dead end into a rural highway. She swung to the right while barely slowing down. As the vehicle sped downhill, she checked her rearview mirror and didn't see the SUV yet.

The car chugged. She kept the accelerator down, but it continued to slow.

"No. No. No. This can't be happening."

She yanked the wheel to the shoulder of the road and hurried out of the driver's door. Open pastures were on both sides of the highway without a single tree for protection. She started toward the fence when a large pickup pulling a livestock trailer topped the hill, coming in the opposite direction of the SUV. Her foot halted midair before she turned and rushed toward the truck, causing the driver to hit the brakes and come to a stop.

Behind her, a red dust cloud billowed at the "T." The SUV.

She prayed the cowboy would help. But she didn't know why she thought he might. No one had ever seemed to want to assist her before. Would this time be different?

* * *

Clive Cantrell locked up his brakes and slid to a stop. The eyes of the woman rushing toward him were huge. He didn't have time to say anything before she disappeared under his trailer. As he stepped out of his truck, an SUV barreled toward him and squealed to a stop. A younger man climbed out of the driver's seat.

"Did you see where that lady went?"

The man's face burned red, instantly causing Clive's hackles to bristle. No wonder she appeared to be running for her life. An older man got out of the passenger-side door, crossed the highway and glanced into the lady's car before joining his partner.

"What lady?" Clive asked. "What does she look like?"

The young man approached him and puffed out his chest as if trying to be intimidating. "Did you see anyone?"

Without waiting for an answer, he marched over to Clive's truck and looked in the cab.

"That's enough," Clive said calmly. "What do you want with her?"

The mouthy man said, "She has a warrant for her arrest. We don't want her to get away."

Clive had worked for years as a deputy sheriff. Not that he was one now, but he still knew something was wrong here. "I'd like to see a copy of that warrant."

The guy glanced at his partner before spouting nonsense about not having to show Clive.

The older man looked across the highway, then stared at him for several seconds. His hands rested on his hips, showing muscular biceps, but Clive kept an eye on the man. It looked like he was covering something with his hand. He wasn't taking a chance that the man carried a gun.

The young guy swaggered toward the gooseneck trailer.

"That's close enough. Get away from my vehicle."

The guy didn't seem deterred, but the older man took notice. "We apologize for the inconvenience. Let's go."

His partner jerked his head back incredulously, staring at the older man—evidently the one calling the shots. The scowl said the younger one wasn't happy, but they both gave Clive another look before climbing into their SUV and slowly pulling away.

As the SUV drove out of sight, Clive strode to the side of the trailer and looked underneath it. "You can come out now."

A pretty lady with honey blond hair struggled to maneuver from beneath the iron beam, and his gaze instantly dropped to her midsection. It could've knocked him off his feet. She was several months pregnant.

"Thank you." She looked back over her shoulder in the direction the SUV had disappeared.

He didn't know her, but he was certain her complexion wasn't normally that pale. "Would you care to tell me what that was all about?" He stared at her hard, trying to get a read on her reaction. Even though he doubted the men's story, Clive didn't know any of them.

Hazel eyes stared up at him as if trying to determine if she could trust him. "I would feel better if you could get me away from here, mister. Those men could be back any second."

He jerked his head toward the Honda. "What's wrong with it?"

"I'm out of gas."

"I've got some in the back of my truck. I can give you a couple of gallons to get you to the store." He considered offering her a ride, but looking at her condition, he thought better of it. She had a husband somewhere, and hopefully, it was neither of those two men.

"I would appreciate that." When he walked around to the back of his truck, she was right on his heels, and she continued to look back over her shoulder toward where the SUV had disappeared.

"You can wait in my truck if you like. I told you I'll not let them bother you." She quietly moved between his dually and his livestock trailer, out of the way, and watched while he put gas in the car. It was tempting to let her go on her way, but he knew better. He had been a deputy and worked in law enforcement for seven years and now worked in his family's security business for two years. This scenario stunk like these guys were up to something nefarious, and he wasn't about to let her go off on her own. "I will follow you to the store."

She opened her driver's-side door and climbed in. She glanced back up at him with uncertainty in her eyes. "That's unnecessary. If you would just point me in the right direction."

He jerked his thumb over his shoulder, indicating the direction he'd just come. "The closest is Country Corner. My name is Clive, by the way. And you?"

"You don't know me."

It was obvious she didn't trust him. Being that these men looked like they intended to run her down to possibly harm her, he didn't blame her. He didn't understand why, but he made certain to stand back and give her room. "I used to be in law enforcement, and I work in the security business with my family. I don't know who those men are that were trying to find you, but I can assure you most people in this area are good people and helpful." No sooner were the words out of his mouth than his ex-wife crossed his mind. Giselle had been shot by an ex-con Clive had arrested. She'd survived, but their unborn baby and marriage had not. What he said was still true. Most people were nice.

She flashed him a slight, albeit condescending, smile. "I need to get on the road."

He merely nodded and got back into his truck. Despite wishing he didn't have his livestock trailer with him, he couldn't simply run the horses home. He went down to the "T" and turned around. It didn't take him long to catch up to her as he followed her down the highway to the convenience store. Country Corner was a glorified convenience store, or maybe some looked at it as a small truck stop. Either way, it was the largest place around for people passing through to get fuel. He parked in the side lot as she pulled up to one of the twelve gas pumps. She ignored him as she got her gas and paid inside. He stayed in his vehicle, looking out for the SUV. When she returned to her car, she hesitated at the door. Even at this distance, he could see her sigh like she had decided something. She pulled next to his truck and rolled down her window. "I wish you would go on home, mister. I should be fine now."

"You're not from around here. Are you in some kind of trouble? Where is your husband? Was one of those men him?"

"No." She practically laughed. "Are you kidding?" It's like she realized what she had said and that her comment made for even more questions. She sobered and glanced down. "I just need to get back on the road."

About that time the SUV cruised along the highway

and slowed, evidently looking over their vehicles in the parking lot. "Get in."

To his surprise, she didn't argue and hurried in on the passenger side. "We can come back for your vehicle later," he said, "but I'm going to put a stop to this right now." He picked up his phone and dialed the sheriff. "Sheriff Copeland, please."

Her hand shot out and tugged on his arm. "No. Please. Don't call the authorities."

"What are you hiding?" He covered the mic with his hand.

"Nothing. Just wait." Fear danced in her eyes.

He didn't know what was going on, but maybe he was better off to listen to her for the moment. "Okay. I'll give you a little time. For now. You're going to have to be honest with me. I will protect you, but I need to know what's going on if I'm going to put myself in danger."

She sank lower in the seat as her hands protectively cradled her belly. Her eyes blinked rapidly as she watched the SUV pull into the parking lot. "I don't want to put anyone in danger, but I'll tell you anything if you'll get me out of here." Her hand waved and swatted the air. "Go. Go. Go."

TWO

Holly clung to the door handle of the large pickup as he steered to the back of the store and around the building. She tried to stay low, although she figured the killers knew she was inside the vehicle. A pickup with a cattle trailer didn't exactly blend in. As they pulled out onto the road, the cowboy kept a watch in his rearview mirror. He was a nice-looking man, in a rugged sort of way. She had never felt so frustrated in her life. Did everything have to turn out this way? She had just wanted a new start in life, a place to call home. A place without drama or trouble from her mother-in-law. A place where she could raise her child. Not even five minutes in the area and already things had fallen into chaos.

She didn't know how to handle this situation. Right now, there was no choice but to accept the stranger's help. But could she trust him with the truth? The older man who had helped murder the couple had a badge attached to his jeans, which meant he was some kind of cop. Cops didn't shoot people and blow up their house.

Clive said he had been in law enforcement. He hadn't claimed to know these two men, but how could she know that for certain? And surely he would have to turn her over to the local authorities when he realized she'd witnessed a woman being shot. And from what she could put together, it sounded like someone else in the house was shot, presumably the woman's husband whom she was supposed to buy the car from. Or...maybe the man selling the car was one of the shooters. No, that would make no sense since he would've expected Holly to show up soon.

Being an outsider, she would make an easy target for the killers to blame. That was one thing she had noticed when she lived in the Dallas suburbs. When you didn't come from an important family or have connections to the area, you made an easy target for people to throw the blame on. One of her friends had been accused of breaking into a used car lot and stealing radios and other things from the vehicles. She'd seen Rod earlier that night and didn't believe he'd had the time to do what he was accused of. But his single mom who struggled to pay basic bills couldn't afford a good defense lawyer, and Rod was left with a public defender for an attorney. He received five years in prison even though the evidence was weak.

Alec, her husband, was dead, and her mother-in-law wanted her baby. Margot was used to having her way and would do anything to take her child. Holly wouldn't give Margot any excuse to take her child. But her mother-in-law was the least of her worries right now. Figuring out how to deal with the men who seemed bent on finding her took precedence.

The cowboy glanced her way. "You need to tell me what's going on or at least allow me to call the sheriff. He's a good man. And as long as you did nothing wrong, you have nothing to worry about." His eyes cut to her as if waiting for a response.

Would the sheriff believe she had witnessed a woman being murdered in cold blood? Instead of answering him, she asked her own question. "Did you know those two men?"

Clive shook his head. "Nope. Never saw them before in my life."

She glanced in the mirror and saw the black SUV following them at a distance.

He looked from the road back to her. "Are you certain you don't want me to call the sheriff?"

No, she wasn't sure. "I would rather you not."

"Are you in trouble with the law?"

That was a simple question without a simple answer. Unless the older guy was a dirty cop. "I shouldn't be, no."

He shrugged. "I guess we will just take our chances."

She saw right through the response. He was trying to make her feel guilty, and it was working. "I don't know who I can trust. Right now, that's no one."

"But you trusted me enough to give you a ride. You need to think about the safety of the baby."

"Who are you to tell me what to do for my baby?" Her tone came out rougher than she had intended. But the fact that her mother-in-law wanted to take the child away from her as soon as it was born rankled. Who did people think they were to say what was best for her baby? Of course, the cowboy did not know this, and the concern in his eyes almost undid her. "I'm sorry. I'm just on edge."

"We've run out of time."

She looked into the mirror. Now they were free from most of the traffic, the black SUV raced closer.

"I can't outrun them pulling this trailer."

She automatically sunk farther down in the seat and laid her hand across her belly. Maybe she had made a mistake. Not only did she not want to get hurt, but she also didn't want to endanger Clive and his horses, or whatever he said he had back there. "You can call for backup."

"I have people I would normally call in for backup, but everyone is out of town. It looks like we're on our own."

The SUV came on faster. "Watch out, mister!"

His jaw clinched as he went around a sharp curve at too fast of a speed while pulling the trailer. The trailer slid off onto the gravel and fishtailed before he got it back onto the pavement. Her heart hitched in her chest. The determination in his expression wasn't lost on her.

The SUV sped up beside him, more between the trailer and the back end of his truck. "Can you not go faster?"

"Won't do any good. We can't possibly outrun them pulling the trailer." His jaw twitched, like he was considering the situation.

A ready-mix concrete truck came toward them from the opposite direction, and the SUV had to hit their brakes and went back in behind them. No sooner had the bulky truck passed than the SUV whipped out again. This time they swung and hit the back end of his trailer, sending it fishtailing. The truck's back tire went onto the gravel again, and this time his truck traveled halfway off the road. A steep ditch lined the road.

She shrieked. "Oh no!"

Clive took his foot off the accelerator as he held on to the steering wheel.

A small size car came from the other direction. Holly noticed it was a woman behind the wheel. As they drew closer, the driver's scared look made Holly pity her as she hit her side of the ditch to get out of the SUV's way. Holly desperately wanted Clive to do something, but she didn't know what he could do while pulling the trailer.

Again, the SUV started to come around him, and Clive hit the brakes.

It was too late.

The SUV plowed into the side of his trailer, sending it sideways. The back of the trailer skidded into the ditch, tilted and then went airborne.

"Your horses!" Her breath hitched as she watched the trailer almost flip over, before crashing back to the ground. It rocked back and forth as the truck slid to a stop, dirt and grass spewing the back window of his truck. The trailer continued in motion, as the tail end swung down the steep embankment. Holly held her breath as she braced for the truck to roll.

Clive kept his foot on the brake as his fingers dug into the steering wheel. The truck came to a stop. He reached into the console and removed a pistol. Her heart thumped in her chest. "What are you doing?"

The SUV had passed them but had whipped back around and was coming for them again.

"I don't intend for us to be hurt or allow my animals to be injured. Get down. Now."

She did as Clive told her. He had stopped on the shoulder of the road as the black SUV came toward them. He got out, aimed and fired.

Holly screamed and slid down farther into the seat. She clapped her hands over her ears. As several more shots rang out, her heart raced uncontrollably. Had Clive shot them? He'd stepped out of the driver's door, but she didn't see him now.

Slowly, she peeked out of the truck. Clive stared down the highway in the opposite direction they were going before looking inside the livestock trailer. Finally, he strode back to the truck and climbed in. "You can get up now."

"I can't believe you did that."

His right eyebrow rose. "I won't be run off the road by those two. I'm taking you to my ranch, and then me and my foreman will come back for your vehicle later. You're going to tell me and then the sheriff what's going on." He put his truck into gear and gave it the gas. The large vehicle revved, and the tires spun as it tried to make it up the steep ditch. He reached down and switched on the four-wheel-drive. Slowly, the truck gained traction and pulled back onto the highway.

"Are your animals okay?"

"A little spooked but not injured."

"Good." The blood pounded through her ears. She didn't know why this had to happen. She simply wanted a job and a new start in life. Get away from the trouble that she had in Dallas. She couldn't go back there and didn't have the money to move again. If she told him the truth, would the cowboy believe her? There was no guarantee he wouldn't think she had killed the woman. As far as she knew, the killers had connections just like her mother-in-law did. The older man was some kind of law officer. They could simply point the finger at her. If you came from an unknown family with little money, in her experience, there was no one to stand up for you.

What chance did she have against someone in authority? None.

"Well?" His tone was serious as he glanced her way.

Her pulse sped up, not only from the close call of the two men still pursuing her and almost taking her and the cowboy out, but also, she didn't know if she should trust him. What was to say that he wouldn't take her to the police or sheriff's department and turn her in. Would they believe her or the murdering officer?

Her husband had all the advantages one could ask for. No matter what Alec did, there were people defending him and believing his word over hers. Her dad had been a decent man—maybe not the best father figure, but she had always appreciated he had raised her. He struggled with his own set of problems, mainly paying the bills and always searching for a good woman. Her dad was not the best judge of character. Holly felt the need to make his life easier by staying out of the way and not causing trouble. Her dad died suddenly of a heart attack when she was fifteen and her aunt took her in. Aunt Camilla was just a mean woman. It wasn't nice to think that way of someone, but she was. Holly had left her aunt's house three months before her eighteenth birthday. She couldn't wait to get out on her own and escape her aunt and Aunt Camilla's three kids. Looking back, she realized it was the need for acceptance and to prove her worth to herself that she had turned to Alec.

She'd gotten a job at an upscale coffee shop in Dallas's downtown business district that not only served overpriced coffee, but also delicious pastries. Alec drove a sports car and wore name brands. He would meet clients or coworkers almost daily and always grabbed a seat in her section. She often wondered what he saw in her. They didn't exactly run in the same circles. After they were married, Alec admitted having married her to spite his mother.

"Ma'am, you owe me an explanation, or I'll have to take you to Sheriff Copeland."

He was right, of course. And she couldn't blame him. "What do you want to know?"

"Why are those men trying to kill you?"

She sighed. "I went to buy a car, and when I got to the

place, I heard people yelling. Then a lady ran out of the house and that young guy stepped out the back door and shot her in the back."

He stared at her. "You're pulling my leg. These guys murdered someone, and you didn't think it was important to tell me? Why didn't you just go to the police?"

"That's not all. I heard more shots come from inside, and then the two men blew up the house. But when they were on the way to their SUV, they saw me. My vehicle had broken down, so I jumped into the car I was supposed to buy and took off. That's when you found me beside the road. I'm not from this area. I know no one."

He repeated, "Why didn't you go to the police?"

"I was running for my life," she shouted.

The cowboy blinked, and then turned his attention back to the road, as he seemed to soak in the information. "I must call the sheriff."

"I knew you were going to say that." Should she tell him one of the men had been wearing a badge? Could she trust him? She drew a deep breath. "The older guy was wearing a badge. If he was some kind of law officer..."

"I didn't see a badge. It was the older guy in the T-shirt?"

She nodded. "Yeah. I don't know if he still had it on or not, but he had it when he walked to his vehicle after blowing the house to smithereens."

He worked his jaw like he was considering the information. "Do you know the names of the people who were killed?"

"No. I have the man's cell number from where we texted each other about the Honda. Oh, maybe one of them mentioned the wife's name but I don't remember what it was."

Clive nodded.

After several minutes on the winding road, with no more sightings of the SUV, the landscape turned into beautiful rolling hills and they eventually reached a huge driveway and a gate with a sign that read Thunder Ridge Ranch. When Clive turned in, she was ready to bolt. Was he just like Alec? This place looked like something out of a western magazine with its wagon wheels and cactus at the entry. Huge pine and oak trees were scattered throughout pastures, and the driveway was a quarter of a mile long. The large two-story stone home sat at the bottom of a valley with colorful landscapes. It was an absolutely stunning place. Holly could only imagine what it would look like in the spring when the pastures and trees turned green. In the distance, there were several other structures, but she couldn't make out what they were from where she was. A massive red barn sat to the north with huge round bales of hay stacked along the side.

Clive backed the trailer up to the cattle lot and a golden retriever trotted up to the vehicle with its tail wagging. He turned off the truck. "Come on. Stay with me and I'll protect you until we can figure something else out. I didn't see the SUV, but since those men seem serious about eliminating you as a witness, they either followed us or will figure out where you are staying."

Dread filled her as she climbed out of his pickup. The man was right about her needing protection. The retriever ran up to her and looked up at her expectantly.

"Is the dog friendly?"

"Yep."

Holly reached out her hand. When the dog wagged her whole body at the gesture, she petted the top of her head. "Aw. Hello, girl."

Three men stopped what they were doing by the barn,

and the older man wearing a cowboy hat and faded blue jeans approached. "Hey, boss. Who's that you got with you?"

"A visitor. We're going to help her pick up her car in a little while. Can you get these horses unloaded and the trailer unhooked? Also, we had a little incident on the road so give them a good going over to make certain there weren't any injuries I missed. I need to go back to town."

Clive took long strides toward the house, and the dog trotted behind him. "Hello, Mollie Beth. Did you miss me?"

The retriever's tongue hung out as she continued by her owner's side. The cowboy stopped at the door and pointed. "Nuh-uh. You've been in the mud. Go help Owen."

The dog reluctantly trotted away.

Holly had to walk fast to keep up. They entered the kitchen, and a pretty woman stepped out wearing jeans and a soft blueberry-colored sweatshirt. Her red hair hung past her shoulders and had bouncy curls. Holly hadn't thought to ask Clive if he was married because he wore no ring, but not all men did. She could see for herself that this lady was an attractive person.

"Hey Clive." The woman turned to Holly and stuck out her hand. "I'm Shaylee."

She accepted the friendly gesture. "I'm Holly."

Clive turned and looked at her but said nothing. She felt kind of silly since he had been helping her, but she hadn't even told him her name. She didn't know what she thought he would do with it. Call her in to the sheriff? Maybe.

"Glad to meet you." Shaylee smiled before she glanced back to Clive. "I'm the cook and help keep house for the Cantrells."

"Oh. Is there that many of them?" Now she felt ridiculous for automatically assuming the two were married.

"Clive hasn't told you about his family? He has four brothers and a sister. And his mother lives here, too. Not all of them live in the main house, but they run in and out of here like they still do." The woman's smile was contagious.

"I had no idea." Holly watched Clive disappear into the back part of the house.

"They all work in the security business together." The woman moved closer, and her voice dropped. Her gaze went to Holly's belly just for a split second. "So how did you meet Clive? If you don't mind me asking."

"He is helping me out." She didn't know how close a relationship the cowboy had with the cook, but she didn't want to cause trouble in case they were in a romantic relationship. Wait. He was just helping her out. Right? If he was in the security business, did he expect to be paid?

Clive came back through the house and paused. "Holly," he said with emphasis as he walked toward the back door. "I'll be right back."

She would have to ask him about the money. She wandered into the living room and noticed all the family pictures on the wall. They were a good-looking family. All of the men were tall and handsome, and the one girl had a contagious smile with dimples. A wide variety of images of kids when they were little up to different stages decorated the room. There were several of a couple that Holly assumed were his parents. It didn't take long to locate the images of Clive. There was some of him as a toddler wearing a cowboy hat and riding a horse. She couldn't help but smile. There was one of him playing peewee football and a couple in his deputy uniform. He looked so different carrying a gun for his job in law enforcement. She had to admit she liked him in this cowboy shirt and jeans better.

"They are a rambunctious family, but they are good people. You will like them."

"Oh." Holly turned at Shaylee's voice. "I doubt I will meet any of them. Unless they will be here in a few minutes."

"They are out of town for the next several days. Hawk, the oldest brother, is teaching a class at a security conference and meeting with a client while the younger brothers, Cash and Sawyer, participate in team roping. They're hoping to make it in the top three this time. Clive stayed here to help keep the ranch running, and he had horses to pick up from a sale. I don't mind the break."

"He didn't mention it." The way the cook talked made Holly think there was something more she wasn't saying. But what did she know? Holly felt like an intruder. Shaylee must be curious about her and her baby, but Holly wasn't staying long enough to get to know the lady. In another time and place, under different circumstances, she might enjoy visiting with her. Just like Madge at the Greasy Griddle. Holly was interviewed by the owner for about fifteen minutes, and the woman was friendly and approachable, even though she came off as stern and matter-of-fact. Was everyone from the area friendly this way? But of course, they weren't. She'd witnessed a murder. The area had trouble just like the places Holly had moved away from. "Earlier you mentioned Clive had four brothers. Hawk, Cash, and Sawyer. Does the other brother also rope?"

"No..." Shaylee chewed on her lip and glanced down

as if trying to figure out how to answer. "Brock doesn't live around here."

That was odd. Before she could ask anything else, Clive returned. "We're ready to go. If you will give me your keys, Owen and I can go get your car."

She needed to get away and that wasn't her car. Not yet, anyway. And she didn't even know how to go about purchasing it now, or if she could find another vehicle within that price range. "I would rather go with you and take my car."

"That's not a good idea."

"But I'd rather do that." She didn't want the cowboy to get any more involved than he already was, but she would feel better with both of the men with her in case the killers had come back. Clive exchanged glances with Shaylee.

Shaylee shrugged with a smile. "The woman knows what she wants."

Clive frowned at the cook. "I want her to remain safe."

Holly walked to the door and called back over her shoulder, "I'm ready."

His truck was sitting in the driveway, and she climbed in on the passenger side. A few seconds later, he opened the back door and Mollie Beth leaped into the back seat before he got into the driver's seat with a slam of the door. His jaw was clenched, but he said nothing. His ranch hand followed close behind in an older truck until they got to the end of the driveway. Clive threw the gear shift into Park.

"I won't do it. You can either tell me what's going on, or I will call the sheriff. No more games. You're expecting a baby, and you have two men trying to kill you."

From the back seat, Mollie Beth leaned forward and stared at Holly like she, too, was waiting for an answer.

What now? She didn't blame him. Was she doing the right thing anyway? Her shoulders slumped. "First. How much do I owe you?"

"What?" He sincerely looked confused.

"Payment. We haven't discussed money or how much the fee is for the protection." At first, the way he had insisted he stay with her made her think he was helping her just to be kind, but maybe he expected her to pay. Of course, he would charge her. It was how he made his living.

"You don't owe anything. I just want to keep you safe. Think of it as being neighborly."

She still didn't quite believe it. "Are you certain? I don't have much money, so if you change your mind..."

"You owe nothing," he repeated.

Holly released a sigh. She'd have to take him at his word for now. "What do you want to know?"

Mollie Beth lay down on the seat and rested her face on her paws.

He shook his head and simply stared at the road for a few moments. "You can't keep this from the authorities. You've got to trust them to do the right thing. My family owns Cantrell Investigations. We can help you."

But once her name was in the system, would her mother-in-law use it against her? It sounded unbelievable, but her mother-in-law wasn't rational and had a mean streak when crossed. Margot Myers had a cousin who worked in the state capital for a representative, and Alec's dad used to play golf with influential people in Dallas. Even after Margot's husband died, she continued to hobnob with those in politics and academia. No doubt, Margot could and would use anything to get the baby. Once Alec, and his brother, Ronan, were telling family stories, and

Ronan mentioned how their mom had gone after his fiancée because Margot didn't want them to marry. Margot had learned Ronan's intended bride had painted graffiti in the bank parking garage when she was in high school seven years prior. Not only did Margot get Ronan's fiancée fired from her current job at an investment firm, but she also found a way to make the fiancée get sentenced with six months of community service. Humiliated, his fiancée had broken off the engagement and moved to another town. Alec had once laughed that his mom had gotten his seventh grade English teacher fired and ruined her reputation.

A sharp ache throbbed across her forehead, and her neck was tight. Holly was exhausted and needed sleep. She had been running around for the last several days with little rest. Maybe it was being pregnant that made her so tired. "I know that. I'm not trying to cause trouble."

"Then why are you making irrational decisions? Unless people have something to hide, they usually report a crime, especially when the killers are after them."

Would he even believe what she told him about her mother-in-law? Even to her, it sounded far-fetched. But she knew the woman. Knew what she was capable of and how she could twist everything. "I realize that."

He seemed to take in everything she had said. His furrowed brow telling her he wasn't happy as he pulled onto the road. The hum of the engine was the only sound in the cab. Fifteen minutes later, they pulled up to the convenience store. "Let's bring the vehicle back to the ranch, but I will have to let the sheriff know because you are not the owner. The intent to buy is not the same thing as purchasing the vehicle. You have no right to it."

She remained silent because she knew he was right. Overwhelmed didn't begin to describe how she felt.

"If you hadn't purchased this car yet, how did you get to the people's house? Where is your vehicle? Or did you hitch a ride with someone?"

"My piece of junk broke down right outside their house, close to their driveway. It has a bad head gasket. I was fortunate to even make it that far."

"You drove it with a bad head gasket?" The look on his face said he did not think that was a smart move. "Your car is just sitting outside the dead woman's home?"

"Yeah." Sarcasm came across in her answer. "When your car breaks down, it gets left where it quit running."

He held his hands in the air as if in surrender. "How do you know it's a bad head gasket?"

"My dad owned a mechanic shop for years. I even helped him occasionally by working on engines. Rebuilt starters and alternators. That sort of thing."

He nodded. "So, you're a mechanic?"

"Not hardly." She couldn't help but laugh. There wasn't any need to tell him, but her career aspirations had more to do with baking pastries than working under the hood of a car. After winning a baking contest, she won a scholarship for a year of culinary art classes and had just started taking business courses when she married Alec. He had told her he would take care of her and that no wife of his should be working. Since her mom had never been in her life, she thought the idea had sounded like fun, like she was being catered to. She imagined that was how a lot of other families lived. When she'd learned she was pregnant, it was like her whole life was falling into place. However, Alec wasn't happy with the baby news. He claimed she'd gotten pregnant on purpose, and that she was putting undo financial pressure on him. She wrote it off as him being nervous and even assumed that was normal.

They pulled up to the store. The little coupe she had intended to purchase was still sitting in the same place.

"Owen, my ranch foreman, will lead the way back to the ranch, and I will follow. But I will call the sheriff on the way. Sheriff Copeland is a fair guy. If you have nothing to hide, there's nothing to worry about."

She dug the keys out of her jeans pocket and got into the little Honda. As far as she could tell, nobody had been inside, but how would she know? It's not like she had any of her personal things inside the vehicle since she fled before she purchased it. She half expected to be attacked again on the way to the ranch, but everything seemed to go smoothly. No sign of the black SUV. The foreman kept the speed down, making it easy to follow. Thirty minutes later, they arrived safely at the ranch. Mollie Beth trotted over to a water bowl.

"Is she an outside dog?"

"Mostly. But there's always a lot happening on the ranch, and she prefers being in the sunshine and being with the other animals. But she comes in some, too, mainly due to my sister's insistence. My mom is a stickler for people and animals not tracking in mud. Not the easiest task on a ranch."

When they went inside, Shaylee had a meal prepared for them. It wasn't much—just sandwiches, chips, veggies, and chocolate chip cookies for dessert—but it was very satisfying. Even the older foreman joined them for lunch.

The conversation remained easy with the others discussing the horses Clive had bought. Holly listened and found it nice to relax and take her mind off the murder she had witnessed and trying to figure out what she should do next.

While she helped Shaylee clear the table, Clive stuck his head back through the door and announced, "Sheriff Copeland is here and would like to speak with you."

A knot formed in her stomach. But she couldn't put this off any longer.

Shaylee shot her a sympathetic smile before Holly stepped outside.

The man was tall with gray hair and a slight belly. Not exactly overweight, just solid and authoritative. He nodded his head for her to come his way. She stopped beside his sheriff-issued truck.

"Clive has been telling me you've had a rough start in our neck of the woods. Tell me about it." His face appeared all no-nonsense but not unfriendly.

Her mouth felt like cotton. She tried to swallow, but it was no use. "I witnessed a murder. But I think there was someone else in the house that was killed, as well."

"Start at the beginning."

She told him about when she arrived at the house and recounted about seeing the lady shot and Holly running to the car she was supposed to buy and the two men chasing her until Clive picked her up on the highway.

"What was the name of the man you were supposed to meet?"

"I don't know. He didn't give me his name, just his address." She rattled off the address. Out of the corner of her eye, she saw Owen move in the barn's doorway, probably listening. Not that she blamed him. People were curious about crimes. She glanced around but did not see Clive, for which she was thankful.

Sheriff Copeland's right eyebrow arched. "And that's the car you came to buy?"

"Yeah. I hadn't paid for it yet, but I had no choice but to take it and run from those ruthless killers."

"Did they say anything? To you or to one another?"

She thought about it. They were talking on the way to their vehicle, but she couldn't remember anything definite. "I don't think so. I was rattled at the time and was more concerned with not being found."

"I'll need a description of the two men and of the vehicle they were driving."

She gave him a quick description of the bald guy in the black T-shirt and jeans, and the younger, sharp-dressed one. And that it was a young one who did the shooting.

"Anything else you think I need to know?"

"Well..." She swallowed. "The bald guy had a badge on his belt."

The lawman squinted. "What kind of badge? What agency?"

She shrugged. "I wasn't close enough to see it."

"Okay. This is all I need for now. We received a call over an hour ago from a local farmer who drove past Tim and Sabrina Mitchell's place and reported the house had burned to the ground. That's the people who were killed. You have no other connection to them except to purchase the car?"

"Correct."

"I'll be back in touch with you. You can't drive the car as it doesn't belong to you. I need you to fill out your contact information."

It didn't look good. She couldn't move into her house until Monday, which was the same day she started her job. She simply said, "Yes, sir."

Clive stepped out of a room in the barn and said, "I appreciate it, Sheriff."

Had Clive been listening also?

Holly watched the sheriff drive away. Things were in motion now, and there was no going back. If her mother-in-law learned about the danger she was in, then it was too late. Margot Myers would somehow use it against her. But Holly would fight for her baby girl and never give up.

Of course, Margot was the least of her concern now because she'd have to live that long first. For once, she'd have to put her concern about her mother-in-law on the back burner. Two killers wanted to eliminate her. She hadn't been injured so far, but next time, they might harm her and her baby.

Clive took in Holly's pale face. Her rapid blinking showed her nervousness, and he got the feeling she was still trying to hide something. He had only half listened to the sheriff's questions, but from what he heard, her account was consistent with what she'd told him.

"I guess I'm stuck asking y'all for a ride into town. I don't have any clothes with me because what I had was still in my suitcase in the back of my car, which is at the victims' house. Do you think you could give me a ride?"

He was certain if the house blew up, authorities were already on the scene. But the truth was he didn't mind going by there because he wanted to look at the scene himself. He had worked as a deputy sheriff for over seven years. After he quit, he helped run the ranch and was also partners in Cantrell Investigations and Security—the family-owned company he shared with his siblings. Sheriff Copeland might not appreciate his presence, but Holly needing to retrieve her things would give him an excuse to drop by the place. "I've got a couple of things to do around here so give me thirty minutes, and then I will take you there."

"I'd appreciate it. And I'm sorry to be so much trouble."

"I don't mind." He watched her walk toward the house. How did he get himself knee-deep in this lady's problem? Especially a lady who is expecting a child. He couldn't turn away from someone in need. Never had. "Owen, let's get these horses separated and into their stalls."

He had driven to Oklahoma to purchase the new stock. A lot of ranches didn't use horses any longer to work cattle, preferring ATVs. The ranch owned two four-wheelers, and it was quicker than saddling a horse. But Clive enjoyed riding when he could. Two of his younger brothers, Cash and Sawyer, were into team roping. He guessed it was in their blood.

Owen and he walked among the new horses—two roans, a chestnut and an Appaloosa. Sawyer had been the one who'd been searching for exceptional stock. Sawyer owned Misty, a fine dapple gray roping horse, but she was nearly twenty and would need a replacement soon. Duchess, the palomino stood with her head held high and sprinted to the other side of the corral when Clive approached. The horse had been purchased for Giselle. Poor horse. His ex-wife had trained the beauty to run barrels at a few rodeo events but had never finaled. Soon, she gave up on competition and quit riding all together. At nine-years-old, Duchess was too young to retire. Clive had considered selling her after his wife left him, but he couldn't stand to part with her. The large buckskin, Binion, belonged to Clive and was six years old and in his prime.

He looked over the four new horses and believed his

younger brother had made sound choices. The large roan watched him with care but stood still while he took his halter and led him into the barn. He was surprised to see Holly leaning against the corral fence, her arms folded over the top rung.

"Those are gorgeous animals."

"I thought you were headed to the house."

She shrugged. "I've always been fascinated by horses, so I changed my mind." She pointed across the yard. "I love that cabin. It's quaint and the wraparound porch is inviting."

He didn't even turn to look because there was only one cabin in that direction. It had been his and Giselle's. A month after she left him, he moved back into the main house, not wanting to see the daily reminder of what he'd lost.

Ignoring her comment about the cabin, he said, "Be careful over there. The new horses are unproven, at least with us, and I don't want one of them to get too close to you." She slightly frowned at him, but he wouldn't have her injured on his ranch. It wasn't unusual for accidents to happen. Animals, even the best of them, could be startled and hurt you. "Have you been around horses?"

She shrugged again. "Not much. I used to spend every summer with my grandma, and she had a horse. Only occasionally did she let me ride because she was afraid I'd get hurt. But I did spend a lot of time brushing him and sneaking him sugar cubes or carrots to eat."

Clive understood that. His sister used to do the same thing. Owen had already put hay in each stall, and he led the second roan inside. "Where are you from?"

She hesitated like she didn't want to answer but then changed her mind. "From the Dallas area."

Owen led the large chestnut into the barn, down the aisle and let him into the adjoining stall while Clive grabbed the Appaloosa. He noted Holly's eyes sparkled.

"He is absolutely stunning."

Her words pleased him, even though many people were partial to the splashy looks of the Appaloosas. "Since you've spent little time around animals like this, let me warn you not to come near them unless I'm with you. They're not pets, yet. These are new to us, so we'll be getting to know each other. Most of the horses are fine, but occasionally you'll find one that's rebellious or one who has been spooked in the past, and things can trigger them."

"I won't get too close."

Satisfied, he turned to go.

"Do you need me, boss?" Owen asked.

"I've got it here but check on the fence in the west pasture. See if you can find where number 909 is getting out. Or send Sammy or Utah to do it."

The older man nodded. "She's always wanting the grass on the other side. Where are you headed?"

"To where the house exploded." He purposely didn't say the people were murdered. Holly was aware of what she witnessed without having it spelled out.

"Let me know if you need me. I'm familiar with a lot of these places around here. I might even know the couple who were murdered and then blown up by the two men you were talking about."

So much for not spelling it out. Once they got in the truck, Holly gave him the address. He put it into his GPS, showing it was forty minutes away.

She asked, "Who are Sammy and Utah?"

"The other two ranch hands." He started to suggest

she'd meet them later, but he figured this might be the last time she visited the ranch.

She nodded. "That's what I thought. I think I saw them earlier by the barn."

Several minutes later, she must have been lost in her own thoughts because she didn't say anything more. He turned on the radio and tuned into a country station but kept the volume semi-low. When he heard her quietly singing along with one of the classic songs, he glanced her way.

She smiled. "My dad used to listen to country music. I don't know many of the new songs, but I know almost all the old ones."

"Same here." He enjoyed hearing her sing. When he pulled up to what was left of the Tim and Sabrina Mitchells' house, there was yellow crime scene tape around the property, and he turned the radio off. A carport sat outside the restricted area to the side, and he noted a blue vehicle up the road.

"I'm surprised they didn't tow my car away."

"I'm sure that's what they would do in the city, but out here, not so much. Especially since you had pulled it out of the roadway." She hurried to her sedan and opened the trunk. While she was busy gathering her things, Clive went to where the debris of the house stood. Yellow tape blocked off the house area over to the carport. The smell of smoke lingered in the air, and Stacy Roberts, the fire marshal, was busy searching through the ashes, while Deputy Kevin Todd was sitting in his vehicle typing on his iPad. The latter gave Clive a nod of acknowledgment when he spotted him and then went back to work.

As Clive stepped toward the carport, his boot kicked a rock, and something pink on the ground caught his attention. He went down on his haunches and saw what looked like bright colored candy kids ate on Valentine's Day that contained sweet messages. But that was no candy. Rainbow fentanyl. A call to Sheriff Copeland was in order to see if they found any drugs on the scene and let him know what he had found.

Clive called Todd over and asked if he could mark the area where the fentanyl was found. He had worked with the deputy less than a year before Clive quit the department, and being that Todd worked in Investigations, he'd never gotten to know the man very well.

A careful search produced no more drugs, but since it was close to the carport, it made him wonder if the drug had been accidentally dropped from a vehicle. He walked away from the deputy and gave the sheriff a call, explaining what he found.

"I appreciate you calling me, but Clive, you shouldn't be at the scene."

"Don't pull that stuff on me, Sheriff. Holly needed to pick up some personal things out of her vehicle that broke down. I won't contaminate the scene. The way I figure it, the drugs were close to the carport and may have been dropped from a bag while being put in a vehicle."

"Could be. Get away from the scene and let my deputies work the area. If I remember correctly, the young lady's car was parked by the road."

"Point taken."

"Cantrell, I realize the lady may remind you of Giselle—her being with child and all—but trust us to do our job."

Clive's jaw clinch. "I help anyone in need. Let's not go on making this a bigger deal than it is." After he disconnected the call, he strode up the driveway to his vehicle where Holly was putting a suitcase in his back seat. Just because his pregnant wife had been shot, didn't mean he was taking this case more serious than any other. The lady needed help. Period.

A glance up the road showed a newer model sedan parked in a pasture, hidden behind a couple of trees. From his vantage point, Clive couldn't tell if anyone was sitting in the driver's seat, but if they were, it'd be easy to monitor the scene. Would the killers return? "Did you get everything?" he asked Holly.

"I did." Her voice sounded strained.

He and Holly got into the pickup, and instead of turning around and going back the way they had come, Clive eased up the road to the car parked behind the trees. The vehicle was on Holly's side of the road.

"Who is that?" she asked.

"I don't know." He snapped a picture of the sedan and made certain the license plate could be read before pulling away. Someone was behind the wheel, but they sank down in the seat.

Holly looked at him. "Why is someone watching us? The two killers were driving an SUV."

"I'm uncertain. They could've switched vehicles."

"I don't like this at all."

Clive didn't either. Holly was quiet on the way back, but he was fine with that. When he returned to the ranch, he would run the plates to see if it led them to the killers. As soon as the thought came to his mind, he realized he should let Sheriff Copeland know about the vehicle, which appeared to have someone watching the Mitchell place.

When they were a mile or so from the ranch, a soft voice said, "There were drugs in the trunk."

Her voice had come out so quietly, he was barely certain she had spoken. "Drugs?"

"Someone must have planted them." She shrugged. "They sure weren't mine. Why is someone doing this to me? Did the killer plant them, hoping to have me arrested?"

"Maybe to throw doubt on your character. But it makes little sense to plant drugs on you if they were trying to kill you. Unless they changed their mind about harming you and took a different approach."

"Can I trust Sheriff Copeland?"

"Copeland is a good lawman."

Her forehead wrinkled in concern. "That didn't answer my question."

"Yes, he's a competent sheriff. You'd be a lot better off telling him the truth than hoping to keep it from him."

Being new to the area and already having witnessed a murder, no wonder she was wary. Unless there was more going on with her than she admitted. Being with child didn't exactly give her the look of a killer and drug dealer. It made him wonder if there was more going on that gave her concern. He pulled into the driveway and when he turned off the engine, he looked her way. "You have nothing to worry about."

Her hazel eyes stared at him for several seconds while she cocked her head to the side, like she was trying to figure out if she could trust him. "That's easy for you to say."

He watched her climb down from the cab. She went to grab her suitcase from the back seat, and he said, "I will get that for you."

It was too late. She'd already grabbed the bag she had with her and was headed into the house. He watched her.

It was obvious she was wary. Not just of him, but the sheriff as well.

He intended to find out what she was running from.

THREE

After a supper of roast and potatoes, Shaylee showed Holly to the room where she would be staying. She turned to the woman. "Thank you."

"I'll be right down the hall," Shaylee told her.

"Oh, I didn't realize you lived in the main house."

"I don't. I live in the cabin on the west side of the backyard, but Clive thought it would be easier to protect you if we all stayed in the same house."

"That makes sense. I'm glad you'll be staying in here." After she put her suitcase on the bed, Holly decided to go back downstairs to help Shaylee clean up. She was tired, but she hated not to do her fair share of the chores.

When she walked into the kitchen, she found no one else was there. She stacked the plates and silverware and brought them over to the sink. Then she moved the serving dishes to the counter and started looking for a small storage bowl to put the little bit of leftovers in.

The back door opened, and Shaylee came through carrying a small overnight bag. "You don't need to help. Go on to bed and get some sleep."

She shook her head. "I don't mind. Really."

Shaylee looked uncomfortable, like visitors were not

supposed to be help. "I appreciate it, but I was going to put my things upstairs. Oh." She glanced around.

"What is it?"

"I forgot my jacket on my bed. It's supposed to be cold in the morning."

"I'll go get it. It's the least I can do."

Shaylee shook her head. "You should probably stay in the main house."

"I thought Clive had stepped outside. You're here and the ranch hands. I'll be right back."

She smiled. "Okay. It's on my bed in the first bedroom."

Holly hurried out the back door. The truth was, she was curious about Shaylee's cabin and was glad when she said she'd forgotten her jacket on her bed. If she lived in a place like this, she was certain it would be fun to decorate. And the beautiful wraparound porch would be sporting rocking chairs or a bench with inviting gingham pillows to sit on so that she could enjoy watching the sun set.

With the three ranch hands and Clive outside, and Shaylee in the main house, she thought it was safe enough to help the cook. When she stepped up on the porch, she was again amazed at how much she liked the little cabin. She couldn't imagine ever living in a place like this, with a big beautiful main home and several smaller buildings. It was like a dream that she couldn't wrap her mind around. Yet she was looking forward to working at the diner and moving into her own home and having her own place, but she realized she would never have much in this world if she didn't do something besides work as a waitress or bake for someone else. Her dreams had mainly consisted of baking, and maybe owning a bakery someday. Then she would feel like her certificate from college would be worth the time she'd put in.

Even what Shaylee did for a living looked inviting. She didn't know how much she was paid, and it was none of Holly's business, but seeking that type of career had not crossed her mind before. It seemed like the best of both worlds. Do what you enjoyed for a career and also be a part of a family.

She opened the front door and was immediately taken with simple but fresh furniture. She quickly peeked at the kitchen and took in the warm blue colors of the mixer, dish towels and the short curtain over the window that overlooked the backyard.

A glance down the hallway showed a door open to her right with what must be Shaylee's room. A burgundy flannel coat lay on the bed, and she grabbed it. The room wasn't that big, but the tall ceiling and large windows made it feel spacious. She didn't think Shaylee would mind, so she glanced into a nice-sized bathroom with a beautiful, tiled shower. When she came back out, she wondered what the room at the end of the hall looked like.

She needed to hurry, but she wanted to take a quick look in the other room to get some ideas of what she'd like to do with her new house. When she opened the door, a gasp of surprise escaped her mouth. A beautiful mural of a giraffe and other zoo animals decorated the main wall. A baby bed not yet put together leaned against the wall opposite. Cans of paint were stacked in the corner. A white dresser stood nearby. Wooden blocks in the shape of letters that spelled out Deacon sat on top of the dresser.

It's like the whole nursery was in the middle of being built.

"You shouldn't be here." Clive's voice made her jump

as he marched into the room. "Who gave you permission to come here?"

She swallowed. "Shaylee forgot her coat, and I offered to get it for her. I didn't mean any harm."

"This room is off-limits."

She felt like a child being scolded by a parent, and it rubbed her wrong. That's how Alec used to talk to her. She stared at him for a few awkward seconds, both of their angry gazes colliding with one another. "You don't have to talk to me that way. I said I didn't mean any harm."

She pushed past him to the front door. What was his problem?

If he thought helping her gave him the right to talk down to her, he was sadly mistaken.

"Holly, wait," Clive called.

She kept marching with the jacket swinging wildly in her grip with each step.

"Holly!"

When she kept going, he hurried her way and caught her as she opened the door. He grabbed her elbow to stop her, but she yanked her arm out of his grasp. "That was uncalled for. You don't talk to me that way. I was just trying to help Shaylee. She's been so nice."

"That wasn't Shaylee's room, and you already had the jacket." He cocked his head at her.

She glanced away for a mere second before she looked back at him. "True. But it's not my fault I didn't know she was pregnant. You could've simply told me."

He released a sigh and stared up at the ceiling for several seconds before looking back at her. "She's not expecting a baby."

"Then I don't understand. Why did you get so irritated?"

"Come with me." He motioned for her to follow.

She shook her head. "No. You don't talk to me that way."

"I'm sorry." He put his hands in the air.

"Fine."

He sighed. "The cabin was mine and Giselle's, my wife."

Her eyebrows drew in as she considered that. "Then, the nursery—"

"Was ours."

Her face fell. "Oh."

"After Giselle left me, I moved back into the main house because I couldn't stand to live in the cabin anymore. The home sat empty until Shaylee moved in. It is part of her compensation. It's understood the nursery is not to be touched."

Her shoulders hunched. "I'm sorry. I didn't know. And the baby—"

"Didn't survive. Giselle took a bullet when an ex-con tried to kill me and accidentally hit her instead. The trauma was too much, and she delivered the baby early."

"I feel so bad. I had no idea." Holly's hand rested on his bicep. "I shouldn't have been in the room."

"It's not your fault. It's probably time for me to clean the room out so that Shaylee can use it for whatever she wants."

Her hand still rested on his arm, but she didn't move it because she felt like he had opened up a wound to her. "I'm sorry."

"Don't worry about it. You didn't know."

She was going to respond, but a click had her turning.

"Is everything alright?" The front door opened, and

Shaylee stuck her head in. "Oh. I didn't know you were here, Clive."

He and Holly immediately pulled away. He said, "It's fine. Come on in. I saw someone in the cabin and wanted to check it out."

Shaylee's gaze bounced between the two of them, like she realized she'd interrupted.

Clive said, "Now that I know it was Holly, I need to make certain everything is secure. You two need to get back to the main house."

After he walked out, Holly said, "Here's your jacket."

The cook looked down the hallway at the open door as she took the clothing. "Did he tell you about the baby?"

"Yeah." She didn't want to betray Clive's trust, but it was useless to deny the comment. Shaylee turned out the lights and walked out of the house. "I loved your cabin and walked back there to see the rest of house. I wasn't snooping. I promise."

Shaylee laughed. "I didn't think you were. I would've done the same thing. It's a beautiful place. Sometimes I feel sad that I live in the home built for Clive. I've been told it started as a one bedroom. Then he married Giselle, and when she became pregnant, his parents had the addition built. They were still in the process of finishing the room when his wife was shot and lost the baby."

Holly probably shouldn't ask, but the question came out before she could stop herself. "How far along was she?"

"About six months."

Her heart seized. About as far along as Holly was. She could only imagine how difficult this was for Clive.

Shaylee sent her a comforting smile before they walked out together. She got the feeling the cook didn't miss much that happened on the ranch.

The woman said quietly, "Clive has gone through a tough time. First with his wife and then the loss of his dad."

His dad? Even though she was curious, she didn't ask what she meant. When they walked back into the main house, Shaylee insisted Holly get some rest. Reluctantly, Holly listened to the request and went upstairs to her room. She opened her suitcase on the bed.

Everything she owned fit in that small bag. The Bible Grandma Harvey had given her and about five changes of clothes, but only three of them still fit. It wasn't much, but it was hers. The things didn't belong to her aunt or to her husband. She hadn't realized they had been getting eviction notice until after the funeral. Except for the stuff that her mother-in-law had taken that had belonged to Alec before they were married, such as the golf clubs that had belonged to his father from years ago, Holly sold all their furniture and belongings. Alec's car had been demolished when he drove off the bridge that killed him while racing one of his friends. The insurance claim was breakeven to pay off his auto loan. He'd let his life insurance lapse months before his death. Holly's luxury SUV was repossessed. She had quickly bought the sedan that had just broken down. She didn't mind not having fancy things, but she was determined to stand on her own and not have to worry about anyone else making all her financial decisions.

If she hadn't won a scholarship from a baking contest, she wouldn't have been able to afford college.

But things were going to change. If she could just get this situation behind her. Which reminded her she needed to say her prayers again. Except for the summers she spent with her grandma, she'd not been brought up going to church, but after Alec's death, there were many people at the funeral. Several people dropped food at her house. Some even called during the next few weeks to check on her. The people didn't know her at all. Maybe they had done it because they knew Alec's parents, but it had a big impact on Holly. She had never had a support group of strangers before then and would like to find a congregation in Cedar Hollow.

After she shoved the suitcase under the bed, she padded over to the window and looked out. The sun dipped low over the horizon, and Owen was heading across the pasture in a Jeep. She glanced around for Clive but didn't see him. She appreciated what he and the others were doing for her. Her heart went out to him for what happened to his wife and child. She could only imagine how difficult it was for him.

As long as the sheriff believed what she had to say, she was going to be okay. It frightened her someone put drugs in her car, and it was obvious somebody was trying to frame her.

Weariness tugged at her. Voices came from downstairs, and she listened but couldn't understand what they were saying. Holly had closed the bedroom door all the way. A few minutes later, she crawled under the covers, and she felt a little better knowing there were people in the house with her. She still couldn't believe it was only this morning that she witnessed a lady being shot. Sabrina Mitchell. A person's life ended so needlessly. The vision replayed through her mind continuously, along with the man dragging her body across the yard and into the house. Her stomach twisted, making her nauseous just thinking about it. The angry voices shouting when she walked up to the house. If only she could make out their words. One of the voices must've belonged to Sabrina's husband.

She wondered what Tim Mitchell had done to anger those two men. Was he into something illegal? Like the drugs someone had planted in her car. Or were the murders simply a crime of opportunity? She had to believe the men had known each other. To blow a place up wasn't exactly a spur of the moment thing.

Holly could still hear Shaylee or Clive moving about in the house. Occasionally a door would close, or muted voices drifted through the house. The sheets smelled of lavender. Much better than sleeping in her car like she had done the last couple of nights. It wouldn't have been too bad if not for the seat belt digging into her side. She showered at a truck stop yesterday afternoon. It wasn't something she was proud of, but it wasn't the first time she'd made do. She'd done the same thing right after she had moved out of her aunt's house before moving into the college dorm. Holly's daughter would have better. She would not drag around an infant to shelters or cheap hotels. If she could just make it until Monday when she started her new job, then she could move into her house. Once she received a couple of paychecks, she hoped to furnish the home a little at a time. There was a variety of furniture and household goods on the same online site where she'd found the car. Even some for free.

Monday was like the light at the end of the tunnel— her goal. She would start her job and get off work by four. Three days. Three days to find the killers. If only Clive and the sheriff could put these guys behind bars, so she wouldn't have to worry about them showing up at the diner. And then she could think about her mother-in-law and how she would handle her. The situation continued to swirl through her mind. Somewhere between the horribleness of the killings and her looking forward to Monday, she dozed off.

She awoke and sat straight in the bed. The clock read 2:34. There was no longer a faint light showing underneath her bedroom door, which meant everyone had gone to bed. The moon shone through her window onto the floor, sparking a yellow glow. Drifting clouds created moving shadows in the room. She got up and took a small sip of her bottle of water, which sat on the nightstand. Afterward, she stepped to the window.

A squeak sounded from somewhere in the house, making her turn and look over her shoulder. She half expected the hall light to come on, but it didn't. She turned her attention back to the window. Mollie Beth ran across the yard and looked out across the horizon like she saw something. Holly knew Clive and the ranch hands were keeping an eye on the place, but her stomach still tightened into a ball. They were only four men on the expansive ranch, three of them farm workers. Could they really secure the entire area? How could anyone do that? She continued to watch Mollie Beth and tried to see what she was staring at.

A light flashed near the barn. Someone was out there. Mollie Beth turned her attention to the barn and trotted that way.

Should she try to find Clive? Let him know that something could be going on? Or was the retriever simply hearing the horses move around? That wouldn't explain the light though. She wished she would've gotten Clive's cell number. Of course, it could be an armadillo or opossum scurrying about. A bulky cloud drowned out the moon, making her lose track of the canine.

Sweat beaded underneath her hair on the back of her neck. Holly raised the window, and a gentle breeze blew in. The air conditioner was on, but since she was pregnant, she slept warmly. If she stayed here another night, she could ask for a portable fan because the ceiling fan wasn't enough to keep her comfortable. A gust blew in, cooling her instantly. Goose bumps formed on her arms, and she shook them away.

A creak sounded, and darkness grew from behind her. She spun. A powerful arm grabbed her shoulder blade, turning her so she couldn't see her attacker. A hand covered her mouth as she fought to scream.

She kicked backward, but her foot only caught air, making her stomach tighten. The hand clamped down harder as she was propelled toward the window. In a frenzy, she fought, kicking until she hit solid mass. Determined to make noise, she struck the wall. She was careful not to hit her stomach and prayed the intruder did not harm her baby.

Someone scooped her off the floor, and the next thing she knew, her feet were dangling outside the window. She clung to the stone sides of the house, but her fingertips could not hold for long.

She screamed. "Help! Someone, help me!"

Her hands trembled as she tried to maintain her grasp, but her fingers slipped. She fell to the narrow roofline below the upper story as her fingers dug into the slick metal, her hand barely caught the edge. Momentarily, the rest of her body swung outward till she was facing the house. The pitch of the roof was dangerously steep. Pain surged through her body, making her right shoulder feel as if it'd been dislocated. Her bare feet dangled precariously over the hedges below.

She glanced up but only saw a shadow in the window before it disappeared. Being pregnant offset her body weight as she tried to regrip the metal sheets. The roof bent under her weight and her fingers desperately squeezed until it sliced into her skin.

"Oh, please God, save me and my baby."

Clive heard the scream, and his heart leaped in his chest. He tore out of the barn for the house. It had to be Holly. He had been keeping watch on the security cameras and then decided to check the outbuildings. Mollie Beth was with him and normally would've alerted him to anyone on the property.

When he ran around the corner of the house, his breath hitched. Holly was suspended from the upper story, her feet hanging in the air. Bulky hedges hovered underneath her. "Hang on."

She squealed.

The gutter bent under the weight, then swung free. Clive got there just as Holly plummeted, and he broke her fall as they rolled to the ground. He had tried to protect the baby, but he didn't know if he had succeeded. Holly was on her side, curled up in a fetal position. He turned her over as he knelt beside her.

"Holly, are you all right?" His hand went to her face, and he rubbed a smudge from her cheek with his thumb.

Her face wrinkled up as if she was in terrible pain. "I... I don't know."

Shaylee ran outside in her bare feet. "Oh, my goodness. What happened?"

"Call 911." He would never forgive himself if Holly or the baby was hurt. His attention remained on her. "Can you hear me?"

"I hurt all over."

"What were you doing by the window?"

"Somebody threw me out."

Panic seized him. He looked up at Shaylee to see her talking on the phone to the dispatcher. "We're going to get you help. What is hurt?"

"My feet and my back mainly. When you broke my fall with your arm, it caught me in the back."

"What about the baby?"

"Fine, as far as I can tell. I'm still shaking."

Shaylee hurried over. "Help is on the way."

"I'll be right back." Clive held up a finger. Looking at Shaylee, he said, "Stay with her." If someone tossed Holly out of the window, they might still be in the house. He jogged to the back door with his gun ready. Where was Owen? He was supposed to help keep watch. Hopefully he did not leave Utah in charge because the kid was too green to handle something this serious.

When Clive stepped around the corner, the security light did not click on. He hurried into the house, careful to make sure no one was around the corner as he proceeded through the downstairs. Once it was cleared, he went to the second story. Starting with the guest room where Holly was staying, he moved in. He didn't see anyone, but there were mud prints on the rug. After checking the closet, he continued down the hallway to the rest of the bedrooms. It was clear.

He pulled his cell phone out of his pocket and hit Owen's number. He said sharply, "Where are you?"

"At the barn. Utah heard something by the barn and went to check it out and called me. Mollie Beth was having a fit."

"We had an intruder. Get to the house now." He clicked

off and hurried back to Holly. She was sitting up on the ground. He glanced at Shaylee before he addressed Holly. "Shouldn't you be laying down?"

She frowned at him. "I hurt all over, and I'm just trying to get comfortable."

"I would rather you lay back and stay in that position until the paramedics get here."

With a roll of her eyes, she did as he asked.

Clive got back to his feet and paced back and forth while he called the sheriff and quickly explained what had happened. The fifteen minutes it took for the ambulance to show up felt like the longest in his life. The two paramedics told them to get back as they quickly took her vital signs. As Clive looked on, he couldn't help but have flashbacks of the night Giselle was shot.

Helpless. Everything was out of his hands. He hadn't been able to protect his wife. Could Holly trust him to keep her safe?

Owen showed up not long after the paramedics and agreed to keep an eye out on the house for Shaylee, since the intruder had not been located. Clive quickly gathered a backup weapon and ammunition before following the swirling lights of the ambulance. There were no more thoughts about if the killers had given up on her. Their intent was clear.

They planned to eliminate her as a witness.

And it was his job to make certain that did not happen.

FOUR

Holly did not feel good. Her heart was still racing. The paramedics had checked her blood pressure, and her pulse showed to be over 130. She knew that was from her being frightened, but it still made her anxious. Holly's ankle throbbed. Her knees stung. Her fingers had cuts. She wasn't even certain what all hurt, but she had pain. She was hooked to a blood pressure machine, and a strap stretched across her belly listened to the baby's heartbeat. Hearing the thump, thump, thump made her feel somewhat better. The paramedics continued to talk to one another in muffled tones. That should make her feel better. Right? Surely if her condition were more serious, they would be hovering over her.

The look on Clive's face was still ingrained in her mind. His eyebrows had drawn down in deep concern. He had moved quickly to break her fall. She didn't know what her injuries would have been had he not been there.

The biggest question was, who had thrown her out the window? It was hard to even think about. Hopefully, the sheriff would believe her now. Surely he would understand only a guilty party would want to go to that much trouble. She was antsy to get to the hospital.

She didn't have to wait long. They rushed her through

the double doors a moment later, and a middle-aged woman with a classy stacked bob hairstyle came into the room. The name on her white lab coat said Friedman. "Let's get you to the ultrasound room and check you out."

It wasn't her who performed the test but a young lady with her hair pulled back in a ponytail. The lady didn't say much as she moved the wand around on her belly. Once they moved her back to a room in the ER, it seemed like forever before Dr. Friedman returned.

"The baby appears to be fine and not under distress. The heart rate is good, and there doesn't seem to be any damage. Besides a sprained ankle and abrasions on your hands and knees, you are fine."

"So, I'm released?" She was relieved.

"Not so fast. I want you to stay overnight for observation. We want to keep an eye on you and the baby, but for right now, everything looks well. More than likely if anything brings us concern, we will send you to another hospital in Dallas where they have better technology. But I don't believe that will be necessary."

Again, that brought the seriousness of the situation right in front of her. Send her to Dallas, to a trauma unit? It would make sense. It appeared Eagle County Memorial was a small hospital. It wasn't like Holly had ever been here, but it being a single-story building told her it wasn't like the hospitals in Dallas-Fort Worth.

"Do you have any questions?"

"Is there anything I should watch for? As in that I should tell the nurses." This was her first baby, and she did not know what to expect.

"If you feel any pressure, cramping, or bleeding let us know. And certainly if you have questions, just ask."

"Okay. Thanks." As the doctor turned to leave, she

felt a bit of relief that her injuries were not worse. But no sooner had she walked out the door than Holly heard Clive's voice. She could not understand what Clive and the doctor were saying, but Clive seemed to be doing most of the talking. Holly only caught an occasional word.

Thirty seconds later, Clive stuck his head in. "Is it okay if I come in?"

"Come on."

He moved to the side of her bed and simply asked, "Are you sure you're feeling okay? Any pain?"

"I'm shook up. My ankle aches. My hands and knees are a little sore." She held up her palms to show him. The concern on his face almost made her laugh. "It's just a few scrapes."

He gently brushed her hand but was careful to stay away from the sore place. "You came very close to being seriously injured. I don't like this, Holly."

As if she did? But she did not say it for the look of torment on his face. She could see he took this very seriously and so did she. "The doctor is keeping me until tomorrow."

"I wish she would keep you longer."

That surprised her. "Why is that?"

"I just want to make sure you and the baby are healthy before they release you."

She studied him. "What were you talking with the doctor about? Were you trying to get Dr. Friedman to keep me?"

"Yep."

He didn't even try to hide his motives. Anger surfaced. Alec had treated her like a child. "I thank you for all the help you've given me, but you've no right to interfere. I'm perfectly capable of talking with my doctor about my own health and that of the baby."

"I just want to make sure they are taking this seriously." He looked at her, and, evidently, could see she wasn't happy. "Don't ask me to not do what I think is best. You got hurt on my ranch on my watch." He turned around without another word and walked out the door before she could respond.

Holly didn't know what she would've said because she was confused at his reaction and was speechless.

Clive could feel his blood pressure rising as he strode by the nurses' station and out the emergency room door. He could still see Holly's glare and tight chin in his mind. She was angry, but so was he. Didn't she know how dangerous this was? He ran his hands through his hair and then replaced his cowboy hat. Of course, she knew how serious this was. But maybe she didn't. Not like he did. As far as he knew, she had never lost a baby before. She had said it was a little girl. She was just over twenty-five weeks along, a week less than what Giselle had been when she had been shot and lost their unborn son.

And it had all been his fault.

His wife was quick to blame him and never let him forget it. Everything in his life had changed in a fraction of a second. They lost the baby. He quit the sheriff's department to work on the ranch full time, hoping to appease Giselle since she'd complained about his job almost since the day they said, "I do." His wife left him months later anyway. The talk around town that had been mumbled under everyone's breath was that Clive should've been able to protect her since Derek Patel, the ex-con who'd tried to kill Clive in a senseless act of revenge after Clive had been the arresting officer in a drive-by, had gotten off two shots before his bullet struck Giselle.

Determination to protect this woman who lay in the hospital ate at him. Not only to safeguard her, but to also give him the chance to prove that he was up to the task.

Should he stay at the hospital with Holly or go search for the person behind the attack? Owen, Sammy and Utah would be watching the ranch and Shaylee. He wished his brothers were here with him. Clive was used to having his siblings and family surrounding him. For now, he would just have to depend on the ranch hands. The sheriff was also a good lawman. It wasn't like he didn't think everyone else was capable because they were. But Clive wanted to be the one to watch her. Just like when driving he liked to be in the driver's seat, not the passenger side.

He walked out to his truck and called Sheriff Copeland.

"How is our patient?"

Clive tried to swallow down his memory of being asked the same thing four years ago when it was Giselle in the hospital. "Dr. Friedman said Holly and the baby are fine. She is going to keep her until tomorrow for observation. As long as everything goes okay, she will be released in the morning."

"That is good news. We're still working the scene and are about to pack up for the night. Shaylee seems concerned about Holly. Owen will stay with her or keep an eye on the house for the rest of the night. Are you going home or staying up there?"

How was he to answer this? He couldn't be in two places at once. "I will stay here."

"Any ideas of who the attacker is?"

"Not yet. Holly isn't certain if it's the same man who

she witnessed kill the Mitchells since she didn't get a look at his face. I have no idea of the two men's identity yet, but you can be sure I will figure out who did this to her."

"Don't go getting riled up, Clive. I know your family is gone and you feel the need to protect Holly. But allow us to do our job."

"Riled up? Someone threw a pregnant lady out of a second story window and…" He drew a deep breath. "Sheriff, you know I can't sit on the sidelines while someone comes onto my ranch and hurts the people there." Clive realized he would never be able to get by inserting himself into what would normally be the sheriff department's job, but he had worked for Sheriff Copeland for several years. Copeland was close to his family.

"Don't make the investigation any more difficult than it has to be. You know that."

"I got it." After he disconnected from the call, he called Hawk and gave him an update.

"Do I need to come home? I can be on the road in ten minutes."

Clive wished all of his brothers were here, but he couldn't ask them to come home. "No, I've got it. Help me figure out who did this if you have any ideas."

"I barely remember the Mitchells," Hawk said. "I have no idea who would want to kill them, but I will ask around. I'm glad you called. I have a lead on the license plate you sent me. It belongs to a man from Frisco, a Dallas suburb, by the name of Hugh Daniels."

"I've never heard of him. Of course, with him being from Frisco, I probably wouldn't."

"I'm checking to make certain he's the same guy, but it looks like he works for Daniels Private Investigations."

"A PI?" This could be a promising lead. "Interesting. I wonder who hired him."

"I don't know. Once I verify it's the correct Hugh Daniels, I'll see if I can learn who hired him."

"Thanks, brother. You don't know how much this means to me."

"No problem. I'll be in touch."

As soon as he hung up, he stared at the security light in the parking lot of the hospital. No one was about. Visiting hours were over, and it was late. The streets were empty except for the occasional vehicle. The whole county was mainly farming communities where people went to bed early. Those who didn't farm we're in related agriculture businesses. The farm and feed store. Convenience stores and diners. Insurance companies that specialized in agriculture. There were a couple of touristy places for the occasional traveler, including fishing supplies and bait and tackle. During the fall, deer hunting was their number one attraction. But murderers, not so much.

Occasionally, someone would have too much to drink and a shooting or a fight might break out. But even then, it had been a couple of years since someone died from violence.

Drugs were uncommon but not unheard-of. The murders were probably drug related. Or it could have been a falling out with the Mitchells and whoever killed them. He sat there for several minutes mulling everything over, and Holly's face kept coming to his mind. The innocence, the vulnerability. A stranger in town who witnessed a murder. And according to her, she was going to be a single mom. Not exactly the easiest thing in the world.

His mind kept returning to Giselle. He knew he had

to let it go that Holly wasn't his ex-wife. It wasn't his job to protect her.

Or was it?

He felt the need to make up for past mistakes even if it wasn't Holly he'd let down. As illogical as that was, he wasn't going to talk himself out of it. He went back through the big double doors to the waiting room. Janice, the receptionist who worked the ER desk, was a childhood friend and had allowed him to go back earlier. He wasn't going to ask her to bend the rules again, but he could sit in the open lobby to see who came and went.

Minutes crawled by and finally hours. Only one person came in, a middle-aged lady with a terrible cough. After she checked in, she sat in a chair on the opposite side of the room and called who he assumed was her husband and asked if the kids were still asleep.

Clive got up to stretch his legs. He heard an outside door open and shut. It made him wonder if it was an entrance for hospital employees. He went to the vending machines and bought a cup of coffee and a small bag of cheese flavored chips. A glance around showed he was alone, and he stretched his legs and back and made his way back into the emergency waiting room. The lady with the cough was no longer there. Instead of sitting down, he walked around the room. Anything to rid himself of the pent-up energy.

"Are you okay?"

He looked up to see Janice staring at him. "I'm fine. I'm just ready to get out of here."

Dark brown eyes stared up at him. "I haven't seen you in a while, Clive. Is the lady, um—" she glanced down "—Holly Myers, your girlfriend?"

"No." That idea seemed far-fetched. He had not pursued a relationship since Giselle divorced him over four years ago. "She's a lady who's been dealt a tough hand. I'm afraid her first taste of Cedar Hollow was not a good one."

Janice nodded. "Oh. Then this is a case for you. I've heard your family has done well in the security business. I was sorry to hear about your dad. Ranching can be a dangerous job."

He wasn't in the mood for chitchat, but it beat sitting there in a chair waiting for time to go by. "I guess you could say this is the case for me. And yes, our family seems good at providing security." The truth was they never would have started the business until his dad was killed two years ago on the ranch. His death was ruled an accident, but Clive never quite believed it although the rest of the family did. His dad was too careful. He wouldn't have fallen off the tractor only to be ran over by the baler. The terrain was barely sloped, not enough to cause an accident. He had retired from the Texas Rangers after twenty-three years. They had always ranched, but his dad was doing it full time, and it seemed to suit him. He looked back to Janice. "How are you doing? You have what two or three kids?"

A proud smile crossed her face. "Four."

That surprised him. It seemed most of the people in their class had moved on with life. He was one of the few who seemed to be stuck on a hamster wheel. "Congratulations. I hadn't heard."

"Randy loves it." She laughed. "I tried to tell him that one of these days the kids would be teenagers and driving, with high car insurance and expensive prom dresses. But he doesn't mind."

"I'm happy for you." He carried his coffee back to his

seat. That was the life he'd always dreamed of. Being one out of six siblings, he tended to think large families were what they were supposed to do. His mom had been wanting grandchildren and had been ecstatic when Giselle became pregnant.

Maybe he should consider dating again. Every time he considered it, a sour feeling developed in his stomach. No desire whatsoever. The thing was, after helping Holly and then hearing Janice talking about her husband and kids made him feel like he was missing out. He couldn't sit on the sidelines forever. If he could just meet someone that he could trust.

FIVE

Holly faded in and out of sleep. About the time she would doze off, someone would come in and check her vitals or the machine. Thankfully, the last nurse had left the lights off but when they came in from the hallway it cast a beam across her bed.

The soft heartbeats of the baby continued to play in the background on the monitor, giving her reassurance that everything was going to be fine.

Every fifteen minutes her blood pressure cuff tightened and took another reading. At least for now she was safe. Again, she must have drifted off to sleep. Sometime later, the door opened, and she waited to see if the nurse would ask her any questions. She sensed the person had moved close to her bed. Her throat was becoming dry. "Could you bring me something to drink, even if it's just ice chips? My throat is parched."

But instead of her nurse's voice, darkness seemed to move across the room. Even though her eyes were closed she could sense it. She opened her eyes just as a pillow was crammed over her face. She jerked and tried to scream, but her voice was muffled.

"Help!" But it was no use. No one could hear her. She jerked and moved, ripping the blood pressure cuff from her arm. The food tray wheeled across the room and banged into a cabinet. She couldn't breathe.

In a panicked fury, she kicked her feet and the covers fell to the floor. Her baby. She had to live for her baby. "Help!" She jerked her head to the left and away from the attacker. Just for a split second her mouth found air and her voice came out. Suddenly lights shone into the room. She slung the pillow away from her face just as someone pushed away from the bed, ran out of the room and plowed into the nurse.

The woman fell backward. "Stop that man!"

Holly got up from the bed and hurried across the floor, but it was too late. The man was gone. A door slammed, and voices carried throughout the hallway.

Clive ran toward her in the hall. "Are you okay?"

"The man." She pointed. "He went that way."

Clive took off in that direction.

Her nurse rushed over to her. "Get back into bed."

Holly padded back across the floor with her heart racing. Her hands were shaking uncontrollably.

A male in scrubs hurried into the room as Holly's nurse said to him, "There's been an attack. Check to see if the man is still in the building or is on the security camera."

Another woman Holly had seen early said, "Let me get Dr. Friedman."

The nurse's hand went to Holly's shoulder in a comforting gesture. "I will stay with you. I need you to relax."

Like that was going to happen. But Holly nodded, not even knowing what to say. Not that she thought any words would come out. She simply was too scared to think straight.

Who would attack her with so many people around? Whoever it was, this proved he wasn't going to stop until she was dead.

***

Clive jogged down the hallway taking his time to glance in every room to make certain the man wasn't hiding. Quickly he made his way down the hall until it ended at a metal door. Clive ran out the door even though it said an alarm would sound. As he plowed through the opening, the fire alarm blared. The parking lot was lit up with security lights, but he didn't see anyone moving.

Tires squealed on the other side of the building. Clive took off at a sprint. Just as he rounded the corner, headlights bore down on him. The vehicle jumped the curb onto the sidewalk. Clive dived out of the way and rolled underneath the tree as a truck went speeding by.

He climbed to his feet and pulled his gun from his waistband, but the truck was too far away to shoot. He quickly grabbed his cell phone and called the sheriff. When the older man answered, Clive hurriedly explained what had happened. "This guy needs to be caught now."

"Did you get a make on the vehicle or a license plate number?"

"No, I was too busy rolling out from underneath the tires of a vehicle. It was a truck, a newer model. Dark in color, but I can't even tell you for sure what shade."

"I will send a deputy that way. If we see anyone going fast, we'll pull him over."

He hurried back into the hospital, but when he got to the door it was locked. He walked around to the front, but it was also locked. He knocked. A second later, a security guard opened the door. When Clive told him who he was, the guard recognized him and let him in.

He hurried to Holly's room to see that she was in bed, her face pale. "Were you injured?"

"Thankfully, no. The guy tried to suffocate me with

the pillow. I don't know what I would have done..." Her voice trailed off, and it took her a moment before she spoke again. "I want out of here."

"You need to stay here until we know you're fine. Unless the doctor changes her mind."

"You don't understand. I don't mean out of the hospital, I mean out of this town. Out of the county. Maybe the state."

The wind was sucked from him. Not that he blamed her. How would he protect her if she wasn't here? He would have to go with her. "I can't let you leave without protection. If you go, I go with you."

SIX

The urge to flee overtook all of Holly's intentions to be patient. She had to get out of here and couldn't—wouldn't—wait until the doctor released her. The dream of putting down roots in the seemingly quaint town of Cedar Hollow was out of reach.

She'd do what she had to do to survive. That was what she was used to.

Clive needed to get out of her room so she could leave.

As if he read her thoughts, he repeated, "I'll go with you."

She knew better than to argue, for he might guess what her plans were and would slow down her leaving. Choosing her words wisely, she said, "I'm tired." That much was true. "If you would give me time to calm down..."

He frowned and paced across the tile floor. "I'm not leaving you alone again."

"I can't rest with you wandering around my room." The temptation to tell him she hadn't hired him to protect her was on the tip of her tongue, but after all the cowboy had done for her, the words wouldn't come. She needed to send him on an errand of sorts to get him out of her room and give herself time to change clothes and sneak out of the room. Pulling the covers up to her chin, she tried to make it look like she was trying to get comfortable. "My throat is dry. I was about to ask the nurse for a drink of water or ice chips when the man came into my room. Could you get me something to ease the dryness?"

He scrutinized her like he didn't trust her. After several seconds, he pointed at her. "I'll be right back."

Even before the door half closed, she was on her feet. Silently, she pushed the door shut and grabbed the clear bag someone had stuffed her clothes and shoes into. Afraid Clive would be back any second, she quickly dressed and peeked out of the room. The nighttime nurse was on the other side of the room with her back toward Holly.

Holly slipped out of her room. Afraid the elevator would take too long, she hurried to the stairway at the end of the hall and carefully kept the door from banging before she hurried down the steps. Her mind raced, trying to figure out the best way to get out of this town with no vehicle. With the cash that was intended for the Honda, she'd be able to pay for an Uber once she made it to Mount Pleasant, a town about an hour from Cedar Hollow. Until then, she might have to hitch a ride.

Once she reached the bottom floor, she opened the metal door and headed across the circle drive to the parking lot, careful to stay in the shadows of the building. Hopefully, the man who had tried to suffocate her would not believe she would make a run for it in the middle of the night and wouldn't be waiting for her. But she wasn't taking any chances.

At the corner of the building, she stopped beside a hedge to catch her breath. Her head swam with dizziness. She closed her eyes and counted to ten. When she opened them again, her head was clear. Clive probably realized she wasn't in her room by now, and he'd be looking for her. Taking the narrow sidewalk, she took off again. Dim security lights barely illuminated the area enough for her to see her path.

A door slammed somewhere. Holly looked over her shoulder even though she kept moving. No one was in sight. An engine hummed in the distance. Another block to go and then a professional building's parking lot sat on the right before ending in a residential area. Her intention was to get to the side roads until she was out of this area.

A couple of dogs barked as she made her way past a brick house with Christmas lights still edging the roofline. A rattle sounded behind her, and she turned and looked but didn't see anyone. Even though the wind was light, rustling could be heard from nearby.

Headlights came toward her from up the road. Not wanting to meet a car, she quickly turned left at the end of the block. A dark sedan drove past.

More lights came from behind her. She didn't have time to make it to the next block, and she stopped underneath a cedar tree, planning to wait until the vehicle went by. But it slowed as it approached.

Holly maneuvered to the other side of the tree trunk to make certain her feet and legs could not be seen. She held her breath and waited for the vehicle to pass, but it stopped in the street. Her heart raced while each second slowly ticked by. What was the person doing? Could he see her? It didn't look like Clive's truck.

Suddenly a light blinded her from outside the driver's window. The driver had a flashlight and was pointing it at the cedar tree.

She took a sidestep and her foot landed on a fallen branch, causing her ankle to twist. Pain shot through her.

She resisted the urge to pick her foot up to ease the pain for fear the person would see the movement.

A hand covered her mouth and pulled her backward. Holly started to scream but then a familiar voice whispered, "It's me. Come on."

She glanced over her shoulder, and her gaze connected with Clive's. Her relief was momentary as he took her hand, and they started across the open yard through the darkness. She tried hard not to limp as the flashlight bounced over their heads and to the right.

Clive said, "Stay low."

They came to the corner of a house and stepped into a narrow lane. A white minivan sat in the driveway, and they moved to hide behind it. The sedan's driver's door opened, and a man got out of car and moved to the cedar. Clive squeezed her hand, warning her to remain still, which wasn't easy since her ankle was throbbing. The flashlight pointed all around. Time again ticked slowly by until finally a door slammed, and the car moved on.

"That wasn't smart."

"Yeah, I know that now, but I thought I could make it." He looked at her and even in the darkness, she could make out his frown.

He sighed. "You're going to get yourself killed. I would say that doesn't matter to me, but it does. Do what you want once these guys are caught. Until then, can you keep yourself from running directly at danger?"

She wanted to argue, but her heart was still racing from the encounter and her ankle pulsed. And the truth was, if he hadn't shown up, she wasn't sure she wouldn't have stayed hidden by the tree and the guy might've caught her. In her condition, she wouldn't have been able to outrun him. "I want to be safe."

"Then stay with me."

***

Clive led Holly down an alley and back toward the hospital. At one house, a dog barked from inside. He wanted to move quickly, but he was careful to keep the pace comfortable for her. She had been through a rough time. All the stress was not good for her nor the baby. If he hadn't caught a glimpse of her from her hospital room edging along the side of the building, he was certain he never would have caught her. But her attacker would have.

The thought of it made his fist clench. He had to get it through her head he could protect her. But even as the thoughts came to him, doubts swirled. He immediately pushed them to the back of his mind. Of course, he could protect her. Just because Giselle had been shot didn't mean that Holly was bound to be shot. The constant ache in his leg where he'd taken a bullet trying to protect his wife was a testament he would do anything in his power to see to her safety.

Derek Patel had been the one to shoot Clive and his wife. One of Clive's bullets had hit the mark, and Derek had died that night. Once Clive learned the shooter's identity, he realized he had arrested Patel some nine months prior for breaking into a lake home and stealing some electronics, jewelry, and a riding lawnmower from the shed. But so much anger over a little arrest didn't make sense to Clive. How could someone throw their life away over six months in prison and a five-thousand-dollar fine?

The incident had cost him and Giselle their baby, and their marriage.

Holly panted for breath behind him, and he stopped. They were less than a block from the hospital. "Let's take a break."

"I'm fine."

"Let's slow down then." She was not fine. He was thankful when she took shorter strides because she seemed to be struggling to walk. When they got back to the sidewalk, he stopped and looked around in search of the vehicle. He was thankful when he did not see it anywhere. "Let's go across the street and up to my dually." A few minutes later, they climbed into his pickup, and he pulled away. He was able to breathe when they were less than a block away with no other cars in sight. He was tempted to lecture her for her risky behavior but decided against it. No doubt, she was running scared. He couldn't expect her to act like a law enforcement officer or even his sister, Emma, who'd been raised on the ranch, served in the Air Force and was around the security business. He assumed Holly wasn't commonly in dangerous situations like his family had been.

"Thank you." As an afterthought, she added, "Again."

"I need you to promise me you won't do that again. I can't keep you safe if you keep running away."

"I'm not trying to sound unappreciative, but you could not protect me at your ranch." She put her foot on the dash and rubbed her foot. "What makes you think you can keep me safe now?"

If she was meaning to stick a dagger in his side and twist it, her attack had hit its mark. "Because I'm not taking you to the ranch."

Her head jerked up. "Where are you taking me?"

"To the line shack at the back of our property. It's in rough shape and hasn't been used in years except by the occasional hunter."

"Will it be safe?" Her eyebrows were wrinkled in concern. "Wouldn't we be better off leaving the area? Like maybe to Oklahoma? There was a place I lived one time in eastern Oklahoma in the country. This time of year, there would be several lake properties available."

He turned right on the highway and kept his eye out for the vehicle. "It's not like I haven't considered the same thing. But my investigator's license isn't valid in Oklahoma. And I have a good working relationship with Sheriff Copeland. I might not get that in other areas. Considering it sounds like these two guys you witnessed murdering the Mitchells were professional hit men, then it might not do much good to go across the river in Oklahoma."

She shrugged frustratingly and put her foot back on the floorboard. "I wasn't talking about staying gone for a couple of months. Maybe just a few days. Give Sheriff Copeland time to gather information."

Or for his family to come home, Clive thought. Once his brothers were back at the ranch, there was no doubt in his mind that everyone would work together to keep Holly safe. No matter how professional the hit men were. "Give me a minute to think about it."

A glance at the clock on the dash said it was almost four in the morning. It wouldn't be long before daylight and more people would be on the road, making it difficult to pick out the vehicle and traffic. Maybe she was right. If they could stay a day or two across the Red River as they hunkered down until his family were home, he could do a better job keeping her safe. The last thing he wanted was for her to be attacked again. When they were several miles out on the open road between Cedar Hollow and the ranch, he finally made up his mind. He would take her up on her suggestion. One of Hawk's friends owned a vacation home in Oklahoma. Even though it was in the middle of the night, he called Hawk and asked him if he would contact Raskin about the use of his home. Hawk told him he would let them know in a few minutes.

He pulled into the parking lot of Griffin's Farm and Feed. To make sure he could not be seen from the highway, he pulled around back and cut off the lights.

Holly glanced up at the sign on the building. "These are the people who are renting me my house."

"Jake Griffin?" Clive hadn't realized the man owned any rental houses. Of course, Clive hadn't seen the store owner much lately except for the occasional delivery he made to the ranch.

"Uh. I don't know Jake, but I talked with Dixie Griffin." She shrugged. Again, she rubbed her ankle. "Would that be Jake's wife?"

He shook his head. "Dixie is Jake's mom. Dixie and Paul owned the store, but now their son runs it. Is the home off of Mackey Road?"

"Yeah. A two-bedroom frame house a couple of miles outside of town."

"Dixie's old homeplace. Her mother passed away a few months ago. I didn't realize they were renting the place out."

"Yeah. I'm supposed to move in Monday morning, if it still happens. Not trying to change the subject, but I can't believe your brother answered the phone at this hour."

Clive shrugged. "I don't think much about it. We've always been like that as a family. We fight and argue but we're also close. Sometimes I forget not all families are that way. Yours?"

"Not at all. My mom died when I was young, so I barely remember her. My older brother spent a lot of time with his friends. We were never that close."

"Was your dad in the picture?"

"Yeah. I guess you could say we were close. And my grandma Harvey was a fine lady. I got to spend summer breaks with her."

Clive couldn't help but notice she quickly got off the subject of her dad. He couldn't imagine not being close to his own family. His dad had been a great Texas Ranger, and an even better father. Clive's phone rang again, and it was Hawk telling him that the vacation home was available. His brother promised he would text him instructions on how to get inside. Clive pulled back out on the road. "We're headed to Oklahoma. This will just be for a couple of days until my brothers come home or until Sheriff Copeland finds the two men. Whichever comes first."

"This makes me feel better, I think. I have a question."

"What's that?"

"If the two hit men that killed the Mitchells are the ones that are after me..."

"Yeah..."

"Then why did the last two attacks happen differently—the guy threw me out of the window and then someone tried to suffocate me. If it was one of the same men, wouldn't he have just shot me, like with a silencer or something? Maybe I've watched too many TV shows and that's not the way it works."

The same question had been plaguing Clive as to why the guy threw her out of the window. That wasn't most hit men's style, and it seemed like he had taken precautions by grabbing her from behind so she would not identify him. She had already seen the face of both men at the Mitchells' house, so it seemed unnecessary. "Sounds like there might be more than two people trying to kill you."

"I was afraid you'd say that."

SEVEN

Holly laid back against the headrest. Her ankle still throbbed, and she was exhausted, but her mind continued to swirl with the events of the night and what her future held. As tired as she was, she didn't think she would be able to get a wink of sleep tonight. Clive's admission that there may be more people trying to kill her than just the hit men, scared her to death. She didn't know how she was going to get out of this mess, or even how she found herself in the middle of ruthless killers to begin with. It seemed so unfair.

An image of her things being put into boxes and into the back of her daddy's pickup truck resurfaced. They were always moving. Always starting over. She had promised herself she would never be that kind of parent. The night her daddy left her bicycle behind was forever etched in her memory. It had been a Christmas present from one of the secret Santa programs in their community. The bike was pink with a yellow stripe and sparkly streamers in the handlebars. It had been a dream come true. She had practiced nonstop for two days, earning her skinned hands and knees, until she learned to ride without falling. Three weeks after Christmas, they had to move again, and her daddy said there wasn't room for her bike. It was the first time she had cried because they had to move. But she had not let her daddy see the tears, for she knew it would do no good. He would tell her that she needed to be strong. Strong became a word synonymous with bad news. A word to despise, and she didn't want to hear it again.

Her dad was not a bad person, but he was a terrible manager of money and relationships. He switched jobs often, although he's stayed in the same industry of working on cars and sometimes heavy equipment. Bulldozers, road graders, that kind of thing. It seemed there was always a job available no matter what town or community they lived in.

By the time Holly entered high school, she stayed at one school for over fifteen months, the longest that she could remember. She had made friends, and the teachers had been nice. But then her dad died, and since Grandma Harvey was in an assisted living place by then, the courts forced her to move in with her aunt.

The only good news was she didn't have to move to a new school again because her aunt lived in the same neighborhood as her dad had.

She had told herself she would not move at every inconvenience and uproot her child like her father had done. Her daughter would have stability.

Doubts hovered if she would be able to make it work in Cedar Hollow. How could she stay in a place where people were attempting to kill her?

Realization hit her that she would've already fled the town if it was not for Clive helping her after she fled the hospital. She was tempted to trust him, but what if he didn't stand by her? She had trusted Alec and that had been a disaster.

Clive turned off the main highway onto a rural paved road, his headlights reflecting from the trees that lined the ditches. Being leafless they took on an ominous look, but she could imagine during the summer it was a beautiful area. Forty-five minutes later, she awoke to crunching sounds and realized they had turned onto a gravel road. She must've fallen asleep.

"We're almost there. After the stores open, I will pick up some things at the store if you tell me what you need."

She looked at Clive. It was a nice thought, but she did not want that cowboy to be picking out her clothes. "I can buy my own."

"I'll let you go with me. We should be safe in the small town. I'm certain there won't be much selection."

"I don't care about the clothes as long as I have something clean to wear. Fashion is not a top priority right now."

"Never thought that it was."

She looked at him from the corner of her eye, trying to detect if the comment was meant as an insult. But he did not appear to mean anything negative. "I don't want to be left alone in a strange place, even if I don't believe we've been followed."

"I get it. We'll go together." He hit a dip in the road and the truck bounced. The headlights shone on a metal gate, and he pulled in. He rolled down his window and punched a number into a keypad. The gate swung open, and he pulled in, the iron bars closing behind them. A pink glow appeared in the east, showing it would be daylight soon. The building looked like a metal shop with giant windows. But it was new looking, and the landscape appeared to have regular care. Tall trees stood in the back and halfway on the west side.

He shifted into Park. "Stay here and let me make sure I can get inside."

She watched as he strode to the front door and then changed the numbers on some kind of combination lock. He was going to a lot of trouble to help her. She knew it was because he was in the security business and probably did this kind of work often. His whole family was involved. But it was new to her, and she had to remind herself that this had nothing to do with his concern for her personally. He would do it for anyone and everyone who paid. Money. The thought of her not paying him still niggled at her conscious. Surely, he couldn't protect people for free. But a deal was a deal. He'd said she owed him no money.

He disappeared inside, and a minute later, returned to the truck. "Everything looks good."

It felt odd not having any of her belongings with her, but she felt safer being away from Cedar Hollow. When she stepped down from the pickup, her ankle almost gave way; the muscle tightened after sitting still. It took a moment to loosen up, and when she walked through the front door, she was surprised to see how open and large the room was. The living room had ceiling-to-floor windows, and the kitchen was connected to it, creating one big open room. A balcony stood above them. He pointed. "Two bedrooms are up there and a bathroom. One has a queen-size bed and the other bunk beds. There is a bedroom downstairs, but I doubt that I will use it."

There was a small stack of wood beside an old-timey Ben Franklin woodstove. He quickly filled it with wood and lit a fire starter before shutting the stove door.

He walked into the kitchen and opened the cabinets. There were snacks such as cheese crackers, saltine crackers, a couple of boxes of cereal and microwave popcorn. "The owner keeps these rotated and makes sure they are fresh. You're welcome to anything."

She opened the refrigerator and noted there were the basic condiments and a few other things like canned biscuits, butter and eggs.

He glanced over her shoulder. "I don't see any milk or food for sandwiches, and the like. We can get that when we go to the store."

"I'm a little hungry right now." She grabbed some instant oatmeal from the cabinet, put it in a bowl, added water and popped it in the microwave.

"I can make some coffee if you would like."

"That sounds so tempting right now, but my doctor told me to stay away from caffeine. I better not."

"I forgot about that."

Once the microwave dinged, she stirred her oatmeal and sat on the metal stool at the bar. It might be her imagination, but he seemed to take offense over everything concerning her baby. "I didn't mean anything about that."

Clive cocked his head at her. "You have nothing to apologize for. So, stop it. Take care of your baby. That's all I want. After you get some sleep, and as soon as we can, I'll take you into town."

"It's a deal." After she finished her oatmeal, she tried not to limp as she moved for the stairs.

He asked, "What's wrong with your foot? You've been favoring it all night."

"I'm fine. Just a little sore." She kept moving toward the stairs, then gripped the handrail for support.

He followed her. "I want to get a look at that."

It was no use to argue. She held up her foot and turned it so he could get a better look at it.

"Really? You're fine?" Using his fingers he prodded the ankle. "Come sit down in the recliner. It's swollen, and it'll do nothing but get worse."

She moved into the living room. When she sat, he put the footrest up and told her to lean back. She did as she was asked and stared at the ceiling, trying to relax. She heard him in the kitchen, getting ice and slamming drawers.

"Here."

She looked at him to see he held a plastic zipped bag filled with ice. She let out a ragged breath, closed her eyes and settled back in the chair as he gingerly positioned the bag on her ankle. It didn't hurt as much as she expected.

A soft touch to her arm had her opening her eyes.

"Are you okay? Is the pain too bad?"

The ankle continued to throb, but the concern in his eyes kept her from saying so. "I'm better. Just exhausted."

He ran his fingers along her arm in a comforting way. "I know you don't trust me and you don't want to, but you have to lean on me. You have no choice. Trust me, Holly." With that he climbed to his feet and walked over to the window and glanced out.

It's like his words had totally thrown cold water on the feelings of tenderness that he had just exhibited. No, she did not have to lean on anyone.

The baby kicked, bringing her attention back to reality—a reminder that she had more to think of than just herself. Holly wanted to get up right then and leave this area for good. She had choices.

A choice to make a good decision or a reckless one. The baby continued to kick inside of her. Back when she was younger, she had been proud that she was independent and on her own. Her dad would leave her alone, and she remembered seeing the faces of people when she said she would be fine at her house by herself. Most nights, she had made herself supper and sometimes for her father. Her older brother, Rowan, spent most of his time with friends and would come in late. Looking back, she knew her father probably left them alone too much. Her brother had gone through several wild years during his high school and young adult ages. Finally, a few years ago, Rowan married and settled down. In the big picture, she supposed her brother had turned out okay, even though they had little communication.

What about her, though? Had she really been so determined to stand on her own that she couldn't accept help even when she needed it?

No, she was bigger than that. It gave her a queasy feeling in her stomach, but she realized she would just have to lean on others. At least temporarily.

Her eyes were closed but suddenly she had the feeling of being watched. Her eyelids fluttered open. Clive was watching her. She tried to keep her movement small so that he would not notice she was awake. For several silent moments, he simply watched her. Then he turned to stoke the fire. Several minutes later, she wondered if she had fallen asleep.

She glanced around but did not see Clive. She sat up even straighter, allowing her gaze to take in the room. Red coals sizzled, and flames danced vigorously.

Where did Clive go? He wouldn't leave her out here. Surely not. He had seemed too concerned about her safety. She removed the partially melted bag of ice. Careful of her foot, she put the footrest down.

Everything was quiet except for the popping of the fire, and the room was toasty.

She climbed to her feet, careful not to bump her sore ankle. Slowly, she put weight on her foot. It wasn't as bad as before. But she stood for several seconds, to make certain.

"What are you doing?"

Holly's heart jumped at the sound of his voice. "I was going to see where you went."

He hurried to her and held out his arm. "I was checking things out to make certain no one followed us here."

"What was I supposed to do, just sit here?"

He shook his head. "I only left your side about three minutes ago. You've been asleep for about twenty minutes. I've been sitting with you."

She half smiled. "Really? I wasn't certain I'd even fallen asleep."

He chuckled. "Not hardly. I was afraid if any of those men followed us, you were going to lead them straight to us with your snoring."

Her leg was getting tired; she leaned on his arm. The throbbing made her want to sit back down, but she didn't want Clive to think the injury was worse than it was. She said, "I don't snore."

"Whatever you say."

"I'm going upstairs to sleep in a real bed."

"Do you need me to carry you?"

She laughed. "Of course not. I think the ice helped because my ankle is not quite as swollen."

"Good. It'll probably take a day or two for the swelling to go away completely. Even though it will probably be easy to twist it again."

She put her elbows by her side and rotated back and forth. "Reminds me of an old hip-hop song, 'Let's Twist Again.'"

"Funny."

She moved too far and stepped on the side of her foot. "Ow."

"Told you." He shook his head.

Not worrying about the charade since Clive already knew she'd twisted her ankle, she hobbled up the stairs with him right behind her.

She chose the bedroom on the right. "Good night. I'll see you in a little bit."

"Night."

After she shut the door, she turned down the covers and then limped into the bathroom and splashed water on her face and got ready for bed. Even though she would have to sleep in her clothes, she climbed into bed. As tired as she was, she thought she would've fallen asleep instantly, but she lay there on her side staring out the window. She got up and checked to make sure it was locked. The thought of being chucked out of the second story petrified her. When she crawled back into bed, she considered what had transpired in the last couple of days. Clive's agreement that there could be someone else wanting her dead scared her, for it made no sense. She had witnessed a double homicide and knew they would want to eliminate her or flee the area. But who else would be after her? There was no one else who would want to harm her. Maybe it was a case of mistaken identity. Or had she made herself a target by someone else believing that she knew more than what she did. It could be someone tied to the two killers.

She would be glad when Clive's family arrived. It's not that she didn't trust the cowboy to keep her safe, but it just seemed like too big of a job for one person.

She lay there for a long time staring at the window, and then the ceiling, but sleep would not come.

* * *

Clive went back outside and brought his weapons in. After the last attack, he made certain he carried backup guns and brought extra ammunition with him. This place had a simple security system. It was not set up to be a safe house like some federal law agencies used. There were cameras on the front and back door. That was it. He assumed there might be one at the front entry gate also, but someone would have to pull up in a vehicle and try to access it to alert the homeowner. The building was solid, constructed out of metal beams, with metal siding. He would prefer that the windows were not so tall and expansive. There was a pool table in the bedroom upstairs with bunk beds. It was great for family vacations but not so much to protect someone in hiding.

When he had first arrived, he texted Hawk to let them know he had reached the location.

He would have liked to have Mollie Beth with him so she could alert him if there was anyone around. But he didn't want to drive back to the ranch, or have Shaylee come here to lessen the chance of her being followed to this location. Besides, the ranch could use the golden retriever. As long as no one had trailed them from the hospital, they should be good.

While sitting in the recliner and considering their next move, he dozed off to sleep.

Sometime later, a creak had him opening his eyes, and he sat straight up. He took in his surroundings before he got to his feet and silently made his way to the front door. A look through the small square glass showed no one outside. Careful not to make himself a target by the large windows, he moved across the room, looking out at the front and side yard. There was no one moving about. No reflection from guns. No mysterious shadows.

Creak.

There it was again, and then footsteps padded across the second floor. It was probably Holly, but he went up to check on her anyway. When he made it to the second story landing, he called out, "It's me. Are you okay?"

"Yeah. I can't sleep."

"You're not hurting?" Concern came over him that she might be having a delayed reaction from her fall.

"Not really." She shook her head. "My ankle is better. I'm sure it'll be sore, but I think I'm over the worst of it. I've been thinking about everything."

"Have you remembered anything new that can help us?"

"I'm not sure it helps, but the sheriff had asked earlier, if any of the guys had said anything. I remembered something."

He waited for her to continue.

"After the woman was shot, a man shouted, 'I didn't tell anyone,' from inside the house. What do you think that means?"

"The possibilities are endless. But since drugs were found at the scene, it might refer to the drugs or the dealer. The Mitchells could be informants or maybe crossed a drug lord."

Holly looked toward the wall like she was considering saying something.

"What is it?"

She shook her head. "I'm not sure and maybe imagining this part."

"Just say it."

"He might have said 'the baby.' As in he didn't tell anyone about the baby." She shrugged. "I'm probably wrong because I wasn't exactly thinking clearly after seeing the woman shot."

Clive considered that. What baby would Tim Mitchell have known about? "I don't know anyone who's having a baby. Well, except for you." A couple of seconds passed. "The Mitchells didn't know you? Right? As in, they wouldn't have been talking about you?"

"I don't know how they would know anything about me. It's not like I told him I was pregnant when I answered the ad."

"That's what I figured." He scrubbed his fingers through his hair. "I'm going to keep working the case like the number one reason the men are after you is because you witnessed the murders. But we'll keep our eyes open to other possibilities."

EIGHT

After Clive left the room, Holly tried to remember exactly what she had heard. But she simply did not know if her mind filled in the part about the baby. It had all happened so fast, and she had been preoccupied with Sabrina Mitchell being shot. Holly had never witnessed anything like that in her life. It still shook her up just to think about it. Several minutes later, she couldn't take trying to recall something that wouldn't come so she headed downstairs. "I'm ready to go if you think the stores are open."

"They should open by six and it's already past seven now. Let's go."

The sun was up and reflected off the frost on the ground as they headed into town. There was a superstore about twenty miles away. It did not take them long to pick up a few new clothes for Holly—undergarments, a simple pair of maternity jeans and T-shirt and flannel shirt because the temperatures were cool. They also bought food to last them a couple of days. Their conversation consisted only of what to buy to eat and whatever supplies they might need. They agreed a second trip away from the vacation home was not advisable. By the time they were on the way home, she stared out the passenger-side window, trying not to think because it seemed the harder she tried to recall things, the more frustrated she became.

Clive asked, "Have you thought of anyone else who might want to harm you?"

"No." She rubbed the bridge of her nose to relieve a headache. "I don't have any enemies except for my mother-in-law. And if the man did shout something about a baby, do you think he could've been talking about Margot, my mother-in-law?"

"I assume since you're asking me, you believe it's possible she's involved."

"Maybe. Margot was a person who'd go the extra mile to get her own way. But murder? Killing someone would even be too much even for Margot. She might have a mean streak, but I don't think she could sink that low. Besides, how would she know the Mitchells?"

When he didn't immediately respond, Holly asked, "Do you think someone else was involved with the Mitchells that may have thought I found something else? Could the drugs in my car's trunk belong to someone else? As in there's more people involved than we know about?"

"When it comes to drug dealers, there are always multiple levels of people involved. Would your mother-in-law try to harm you even though you're pregnant with her grandbaby?"

A tingling went down Holly's spine. "I don't think so. I don't think she would mind harming me, but she wants Alec's baby." Of course, Holly had never went against the woman until she told her mother-in-law she wouldn't consider giving the child up.

"What if she believes she won't gain custody of the child? Do you think she would harm you to get even? If I can't have the child, then neither will you sort of thing."

"It's a terrible thought." Holly gently rubbed her belly. "It's far-fetched. Besides, there was no way for Margot to know I was meeting Tim Mitchell to purchase the car. I didn't tell anyone where I was moving."

Clive looked at her. "Seriously. No one?"

Holly thought for a moment. "I may have mentioned moving to Rachael, a lady from church where my late husband Alec grew up worshipping. But I didn't specify the town of Cedar Hollow. Just that I was moving northeast of Dallas." She considered that for a moment. Would the woman tell Margot? Maybe.

"What about having your mail forwarded? Have you already taken care of that?"

"Of course. That must be it." She sighed. "I filled out the form at the post office after my interview with Madge at Greasy Griddle, and I put down my deposit on the rental house before I left on Wednesday. I wonder if Margot knows someone at the post office who would let her know."

Clive said, "I have hard time believing anyone would go to such measures to harm an expectant mother. But I've seen terrible things in my life. A man had shot at me even though my pregnant wife was beside me on the sidewalk."

"You're right," Holly said with a sigh.

"When we get back to the house, I would like any information you can give me on Margot. Anything that would help us track her down to see who she might use or if she has anything in her background that would lead us to the killers."

"I can do that." Holly still struggled to believe she might be involved, but there was one thing she did know. They might not survive the next attack and needed to learn the truth now.

* * *

Clive was relieved when they arrived back at their vacation home safely. He had kept a constant lookout for any suspicious vehicles but saw none that concerned him.

When he killed the engine in the driveway, Holly said, "I'm glad we made it safely. I don't believe I could take another attack this morning."

"I know what you mean." Making the decision to leave Texas had seemed simple, and he knew that there was a good chance they made it out of Cedar Hollow without being spotted. Between last night and this morning, he continuously ran the scenarios through his mind, considering his options. He fully believed he could keep Holly safe on his own. Sheriff Copeland and his deputies were good, but didn't have much experience with personal, one-on-one security like his family did. When Derek Patel drove by and starting shooting at him and Giselle, the shootout was over before the first deputy had stepped out of the building. It had only taken seconds, but it still bothered him that the man was brazen enough to attack him while Clive was stepping out of the sheriff's department. He concluded it was better off to stay here at the vacation house until his family returned home. "Let me check the house out before you go inside. Here's the keys." He handed them to her.

She gave him a faint smile. "Hurry."

He tried not to make her nervous since he knew she'd already gone through a big ordeal, but he needed to let her know where they stood. "If anything should happen, take my truck and leave. Call Hawk. Here is his number." She glanced at the piece of paper he had left on the console before he exited the vehicle. He'd left her the phone numbers of all of his siblings. A look around at the surroundings showed nothing had changed since they had left that morning, but he knew things were not always as they appeared. He disarmed the alarm when he went through the door and carefully checked out the rooms, including closets and the walk-in pantry.

He strode back outside and said, "All clear. If you want to go in, I can grab these things."

"I don't mind." They both filled their arms with the items they had bought and went through the front door, placing all the groceries on the counter. He found himself smiling. Holly might be vulnerable considering she was six months pregnant, but she didn't like him trying to do everything for her.

He had bought a couple of backup flashlights while at the store, but he had put them in the back pocket of the driver's seat. "I didn't get the flashlights. I'll be right back."

He'd just stepped up to his truck when something glistened from the trees, catching his attention.

A shot rang out.

His weapon was in his hand before his knee hit the ground behind the large vehicle. He took aim and fired.

Another shot rang out, hitting the bumper just in front of him. He squeezed the trigger again. Movement flashed between the trees. He readied to fire, when the sound of a boot on gravel came from behind him. He swung around and shot a man twenty yards behind him. The man fell to the ground.

Clive looked around for the man in the woods, but he didn't see him. He got to his feet and edged to the back side of his vehicle. He looked around the tailgate, careful to stay protected. In the distance, the man sprinted out from the brush before vanishing again. The loud rumble of an engine interrupted the silence before speeding away.

He hurried over to the fallen man just as the front door to the home cracked open. He turned to see Holly standing behind the protection of the metal door. He hollered, "Get back inside and call 911."

"Is he alive?"

Clive felt for a pulse but there was nothing there. "No. We'll need the sheriff's department."

Clive hadn't wanted to kill anyone, but he had been left with little choice.

"That's one of the hit men! The one who shot Sabrina Mitchell."

Clive turned to see Holly standing behind him staring at the dead man, her face white as a sheet.

A wave of irritation descended on him. How did these guys keep finding them? What would've happened to Holly if the guy had shot Clive as soon as he stepped out of the house?

NINE

Holly felt sick. She had only seen dead people at funerals after they were cleaned up and looking like they were sleeping peaceably. Nothing like today with the man's body contorted and his arm flung unnaturally out to the side. She looked away.

Her nerves were on edge, making her feel shaky and unstable. Under normal circumstances this would have shaken her up, but being pregnant made her physical reaction even worse. Morning sickness had gone away after the third month, but right now the nausea was back. She reentered the house and went straight to the bathroom, where she got sick. Then she went into the living room and stared out the window but purposely did not look at the man's face. As if Clive was aware of her watching him, he returned inside.

"Get ready to go. We won't be staying here anymore because our position has been compromised. No doubt the man who got away will let the top dog know where we are."

"I'll pack the food that we already bought." She moved to the kitchen and quickly started stuffing their groceries back into the bags.

Clive followed her. "You recognized the victim. Right?"

"Yeah. He was the young man who shot Sabrina Mitchell. You should also recognize him since you saw them on the side of the road when I first met you." She stuffed the snacks into the bag and looked around to make sure she hadn't missed anything.

"Just making sure we were on the same page. Could he also be the same man who tried to suffocate you in your hospital room?"

"I... I don't know. Maybe. I didn't get a good look at him." Suddenly she recalled when she shoved the pillow away from her face and found her voice. She glanced back at the body on the ground outside and noted his black shoes. "If he was the one in the hospital attack, then he changed shoes. That man was wearing white running shoes, not black."

Clive's eyebrows furled as a look of concern crossed his face. "I hope you're wrong. If not, then that confirms there are at least three people that have attacked you."

Sirens sounded in the distance as two deputy trucks and a white SUV pulled down the long driveway. Clive turned to her. "We'll be leaving as soon as they're done questioning us. Feel free to stay inside until they need to talk to you." He walked out the door to greet the deputies.

Holly was ready to get out of here and get back on the road to another location. The fact that they found her again baffled her. How did they keep finding her?

Had they put some kind of tracker on one of them?

She quickly went back through the house, checking to make sure they had gathered all of their items. Even though the men had found them and knew where they stayed, she didn't want anyone finding any more evidence to lead them to their next location. She went back upstairs and went through her room to grab the clothes she had worn yesterday. When she returned downstairs, she put them in a bag and gathered the rest of the food bags and walked out the front door. A man with the word Coroner in bright yellow letters on his jacket was bent over the dead man.

Clive motioned her over. She joined him and set the bags at her feet and folded her arms around herself to keep warm. She turned her back on the victim so she wouldn't be distracted. The older deputy, a man with gray hair and a slight paunch, said, "Tell me what happened."

Holly wasn't even certain where to begin or what all Clive had told them. She started from the beginning. "I was moving to Cedar Hollow, Texas, to start a job when my car started giving me trouble. I found a car for sale online in the area and went to meet the seller at his house. But when I arrived, there was yelling going on in the house and then a lady ran out of the back door and a man shot her in the back. I believe he—" she nodded her head in the direction of the body "—was the shooter."

A look of mild surprise showed on the deputy's face, but he didn't say anything besides, "Go on."

She continued to tell the story all the way up until the men had showed up at the vacation home and what had transpired just a few minutes ago. She tried to keep her answers short after she realized Clive must not have started at the total beginning with the trouble at Cedar Hollow.

The deputy asked several more questions and then told her he was done for now. She grabbed her bags and loaded them into Clive's warm truck and climbed inside. He must have started it for her with the key fob, and she was glad the heat was on high. She wondered if her answers had created more questions from the deputies.

Five minutes later, the lawmen walked off toward their vehicle, and Clive climbed into his truck. When he buckled, she asked, "Should I not have told them about what happened in Cedar Hollow?"

He shook his head. "It does not matter. I had abbreviated that part for time's sake, but it's not like the deputy wouldn't have access to all the information after the official report is completed in Cedar Hollow."

"You like to keep this case close and not share information. Don't you?"

His right eyebrow arched as he gave her a glassy stare. "You mentioned the older man was wearing a badge. I doubt anyone in this sheriff's department is involved, but you never know how wide of a loop the dealers have thrown."

"What does that mean?"

He shook his head. "There could be more people involved, even more people in law enforcement."

Why didn't he just say so? Clive must live a lonely life doing everything on his own. But what was she thinking? She'd spent most of her life doing the same and when she'd trusted in her husband, it hadn't turned out well. "What will the deputies and investigators do now?"

"The victim will be transported to the morgue. Hopefully, we will learn his identity soon, even though he had no identification on his person."

"Are you allowed to leave town? As in did the deputies ask you to stay in the area?"

He glanced at her. "No, officers don't tell you not to leave town unless they are charging you with a crime. That's a Hollywood thing."

"I didn't realize that," she said.

Once the deputies had left the yard, Clive got out one last time to say he was going to check on the house. After a minute, he returned to the truck. "Looks like we got everything."

A deep weight rested on her shoulders as she did not know what they could do to get out of the situation. She asked, "Where to now?"

"We're going back to Cedar Hollow to get some answers once and for all."

She was afraid he was going to say that.

Even before Holly had asked the question of where they should go, Clive debated what the next move should be. Honestly, he didn't know if going back was the smartest decision. The deputies here in Oklahoma had been professional and would dig deeper into the story. Being that he was just in security and no longer a law officer, they could try to charge him with the killing of the man. They reassured him they would contact Sheriff Copeland to let the department know the identity of the shooting victim.

"Is Shaylee okay?"

"As far as I know. We need to stop and get a couple of burner phones. It bothers me that these guys found us."

"Do you think you have a tracker on your vehicle?" she asked.

"I don't think so, but I am beginning to wonder. I want you to turn your phone off."

"But I haven't been using it. Is there a way for them to track me?"

"Possibly. Until we know how they are finding us we need to take every precaution." His brothers were more tech savvy than Clive, but it always amazed him how people could use GPS or some other method for tracking. Since the killing of the Mitchells appeared to be a professional hit, there was no telling what resources the one at the top had. Holly had not carried any items with her from her vehicle that he knew of. "Do you have anything on you, like in your pockets or something that you're carrying that could have a tracker on it?"

She frowned. "No. Just my small backpack. I use it as a purse that has my money in it."

"Is there any way it could have been left alone where one of the killers could've put something in it?"

"I don't think so. Not unless the guy put it in there when he was in my hospital room. Or maybe after he threw me out the second story window. But he had disappeared so fast I doubt he had time."

"You're right. He would have had to preplan that and know exactly what he was looking for. Seems unlikely, but I don't want to rule anything out." Someone must've put something on his truck. It was a feasible explanation. Since the man was at the ranch, his truck would've been the easiest place for that. Or someone knew what vehicle he was driving while it was parked at the hospital. He would have to have his vehicle searched.

"I need to call my brothers and let them know what is going on."

She nodded.

He called Cash this time since he should be done with his team roping competition.

"What's happening?"

Clive said, "I've got you on speaker and Holly's with me." He briefly explained what had happened at the vacation rental.

"You must be being tracked," Cash warned. "You might want to get a couple of burner phones."

"Already planned on stopping at the first place we come to and buy some. I'll text you with our numbers."

"I'm coming home. Don't try to talk me out of it."

His brother's words reminded him of why he liked to work with family. They were dependable. "How did you and Sawyer do at the rodeo?"

"We got third overall, so we're in the money. In the final round, Sawyer got the head right out of the gate, but it took me an extra step to get my loop on him. Don't try and change the subject. Sawyer and I will head out now in Mom's vehicle. After the conference, Hawk can drive the horse trailer home and take Emma and Mom with him."

"I appreciate it, but we still have a business to run. Are y'all through with the classes at the conference? Did Hawk meet with the senator?"

"The classes are not over until the morning. Now that the roping competition is completed, Sawyer and I were planning on being at the conference, but we can skip it. Hawk meets with the senator tonight."

"Stay. I can hold down the fort until you all get back."

"Holly, he's always been stubborn." His brother changed tactics, opting to talk to his passenger didn't surprise him. "Don't you worry. Hunker down, and all the Cantrells will be home tomorrow."

She blinked at Clive, and he wasn't certain if she'd respond.

She said, "I'm glad to hear that. He likes to pretend he has it all under control."

Cash had the nerve to chuckle. "You got that right."

"Funny." What did they prefer him to do? Sit on his hands until the cavalry arrived? It was time to get this conversation back to a serious note. "I'll see you all tomorrow night, and if anything else happens, I'll let you know."

"Oh, before you go. Emma wants to make certain you're taking care of Mollie Beth."

He impatiently drummed his fingers on his thigh. "I am. Mollie's on the ranch with Shaylee. Tell her we're not totally incompetent."

"Little sister will be glad to hear it."

A couple of minutes after disconnecting, Holly said, "I think I would like your family. Where does you sister fall in the middle of all you brothers?"

"Emma is the next to the youngest, number five."

"Does she and your mom work in the security business, too?"

He drew a breath and sat straighter in his seat. The truth was, she tried to do a lot more than what the brothers were happy with, and she didn't take to being protected by them. "Yeah, Emma does. But being one of the youngest, she's not as active in the business as the brothers. Mom helps out here and there when needed, mainly in support. She enjoys watching my brothers participate in team roping."

Clive thought his mom was still struggling to find meaning since his dad died. Recently, she got up early in the morning to run. It was probably a phase she was going through.

Holly seemed to accept that answer with a nod. If Emma would've heard Clive's statement, she would've given him an earful. His sister had wanted to do everything her brothers could do. It surprised all of them when their dad supported her decision to join the air force. She'd learned to train K-9s for military use, which was much better than their sister being in combat. He was glad she had decided not to reenlist, preferring to work with the family after their father died.

When they crossed back over the Red River and entered Texas, Clive felt better about being closer to home, but he stayed earnest about looking for the SUV the two assassins had driven and the car that had followed Holly when she fled the hospital. At this point, he didn't even know what he was looking for since there had been so many attacks. Which brought up the question again of how big the operation was. Who was behind the attacks? It wasn't like there was big crime in rural Eagle County, but rather most of the cases he had learned about were through trainings or through the grapevine in the sheriff's department. It was rare to have more than one or two hit men on a case, except for very large, organized crime deals. If they had something like that going on in Eagle County, the sheriff needed to be on top of it and maybe even seek outside agencies for assistance.

He glanced over at Holly. Her head lay against the headrest, and her face was pointed toward the window. Whether her eyes were closed or if she was watching the scenery go by, he didn't know. He was glad she did not press him on where they were going because he needed time to consider his actions.

Two minutes later, he drove past a large truck stop but continued driving. A quick glance showed there was neither the SUV nor the white car in the parking lot. It meant little considering it would be easy for someone to park in the back, making it impossible for him to see it.

Shaylee or Owen would have called if something was going on, but Clive punched his foreman's number anyway. When the older man answered, Clive asked, "Any trouble?"

"It's been quiet, or I would've let you know. Sammy and Utah helped me. I had to fuss at Utah for being on his phone. Besides that, all the work is going smoothly. The new stock are all eating, and Sammy led them around then corral, getting them used to everything. So far, they all seem well trained. The winter wheat is up even after we planted it late. When can I expect you back?"

Clive didn't want anyone to know where they were until he learned more of what was going on. That way if Owen or Shaylee was questioned, they could honestly give the truthful answer. "I don't know yet. Just keep an eye on things, and I'll let you know if we need anything."

Holly sat up straight in the passenger seat. "How come we didn't stop?"

"Because I wanted to check to make certain the truck or SUV any of the guys were driving wasn't there before we stopped." He went down the highway until he came to an off-ramp and exited. Then he turned the truck around and went back to the truck stop. He pulled in and drove to the back of the building. Multiple semitrucks were parked in a straight line, and three more were at the pumps. Only two vehicles, a white cargo van and a faded sports car that had seen better days, were parked among the big rigs. He pulled up to the building.

"Come on in with me."

"Good. I need something to eat."

They were in the large store for less than five minutes. Clive bought two burner phones and a couple of hot dogs and chips. When they got back in the pickup, he said, "Check your cell one last time and jot down any numbers you might need. We'll be leaving our cells off until these guys are arrested. I'm only going to let my family and the sheriff know my new number. Don't share your number with anyone but me."

She nodded.

After he'd sent his number out with his new phone, he handed her half of the food. He put his portion on the console and shifted his truck into gear.

"Mmm. I'm going to eat before I jot down a couple of numbers."

He nodded and took a big bite before pulling out on the highway. They ate in silence while he merged into traffic.

"Are you going to call the sheriff or is the text enough?"

He cocked his head at her. "I'll call him in a bit."

A smile slowly appeared. "I get the feeling you're having to convince yourself to give him a call. And you don't like being questioned."

"Nope. Not one bit." He didn't even consider denying it. A look her way said she enjoyed his admission. He popped the last chip in his mouth and wadded up the trash and put it in the bag.

She turned to him with her eyebrows raised. "You told me yesterday I could trust him..."

"I don't like asking for help. But Sheriff Copeland needs to be more involved. He is one person I mostly trust."

"Now, you're starting to sound like me after my husband admitted that he married me to get even with his mom and prove she didn't control him. Now I don't believe anyone. Why don't you trust the sheriff? Did he do something? Or do you save that honor for family members only?"

He realized she had just made a big admission, and he started to answer her, but didn't want to go down that path.

"What aren't you saying?" she asked.

He shrugged. "It's not a big deal. After my dad died, I wasn't happy when the sheriff said he believed it was accident. I thought his death should've been investigated more. I had quit the department two and half years earlier, so I suppose I lost my persuasion power."

She sat straight in the seat, and her voice softened. "How did your dad die?"

"On the ranch." He hadn't talked about his dad in over a year with anyone. He was tired of everyone telling him he should drop it. "He was moving round hay bales with the tractor. There's an incline on the south pasture where we raise alfalfa. It appears the tractor tilted, making Dad fall off and then he was run over by the baler."

"I'm so sorry." Her hand went to her mouth. "That must've been horrible."

He swallowed. It was. Clive had been the one to find his father's body, and he was the only family member besides maybe his mom who doubted it was an accident. His dad had been distracted the couple of days before his death. There was no one as careful as his dad. During his career as a Texas Ranger, Deacon Cantrell had seen many terrible things. He constantly warned his kids to pay attention to what they were doing so they wouldn't get hurt. His dad had raised hay on that pasture for years. Clive didn't believe Deacon Cantrell had suddenly become careless.

"What did you want the sheriff to do?" Holly's voice interrupted his thoughts.

"Looking into Dad's death would've been nice. Did I mention the tractor wasn't running?"

"I don't get it." She shrugged.

"How did the tractor run over my dad if it wasn't running?"

"Maybe it ran out of gas."

"Diesel," he corrected her. "The tractor had fuel. It's always bothered me the day before his 'accident' he'd come down harsh on me for coming into his office. Dad told me to help Emma feed the animals. It was winter, which always took longer to tend to feed because grass is limited. But Cash had already helped her, and they were done when I went to help. I stepped into Dad's office to ask him about borrowing his truck to take to town since mine had a flat tire. Dad quickly closed his laptop and snapped at me to do what I was told and don't make him repeat himself. If you knew my dad, you would understand this was out of character for him." At the time, instead of being concerned, it had made Clive mad to be talked to like he was a child. It wasn't until the next day after finding his dad's body that he began to question if something more had been going on that had upset him.

Her cell phone dinged, saving him from answering the question. It surprised him since she hadn't received a call or text since he'd met her. His eyes lifted to hers to gauge her reaction.

"I don't recognize the number." Her gaze narrowed as she stared at the text. She flashed her phone toward him so he could read it. "It's about my rental house."

I know this is late notice, but I need you to sign another paper on the rent if you want to take it on Monday. Meet me at the feed store. Okay?

Clive looked at her. "When were you supposed to meet Dixie to get the keys to the house?"

"We didn't really talk about it. I assumed I would get it on Monday after I got off work because she asked me what time I got off. But that's just my assumption. We had agreed on the amount online. I haven't even looked at the inside of the home except in pictures. On my first night when I drove through Cedar Hollow, I drove past it. I may have got out and looked into the windows." She smiled.

He thought about it for a second because it sounded odd that Dixie would want to meet her at the feed store. "There's been no talk about the feed store before in your communication?"

She shook her head no. "I guess I didn't have everything planned out too well, as far as making everything official. I got distracted when my car started giving me problems. But when I talked to Dixie on the phone, she seemed nice, and I had no reason to doubt her."

"Your instincts were correct. Dixie is a good lady whom you can trust. She's been in the area for a long time. Like I said earlier, most people are very good around here, Paul and Dixie Griffin included." It still struck him as strange that Dixie would pick tonight to meet Holly with the keys. He glanced back to the text message and noted the phone number. He didn't have the woman's number saved in his contact list.

"You don't think it's legit?" she asked.

"The area code isn't Cedar Hollow's. That doesn't mean that Dixie doesn't have a number from outside the area because it's possible, but I'm not buying it."

Holly gently rested her hand on her belly. "Do you want me to leave my cell phone on or turn it off?"

"Leave it on for now in case the person texts you again."

She nodded. "If it's not Dixie setting up the meeting, then why the feed store?"

"I don't know." That was bugging Clive, too. "Have you spoken with Jake Griffin?"

"No. Except for the night we parked at the store, and you mentioned him, I'd never heard of the guy's name. Why, what's bothering you?"

"Everything," Clive admitted honestly. "We don't have much to go on to solve this case. We don't have many leads, and I don't trust anyone. It may be Dixie contacting you, or Jake. Or someone totally different. It's common for criminals to use burner phones. It could also be your mother-in-law, since she wouldn't be familiar with places in the area. She could have someone meet you at the feed store because she doesn't know anywhere better."

"Could be Margot." Holly nodded. "If the person texting is not Dixie, then I believe it's one of the hit men. Well, there's only one of them left."

"The latter does seem the most credible. I'll get Shaylee and the ranch hands to stay with you when I go to the feed store. If everything is clear—"

"I'm going with you," she said, cutting him off.

He didn't like it, because he didn't know how he would keep her safe while also making certain it wasn't a setup. "You know we could be walking into one of the gunman's traps."

"Do you need to call the sheriff?"

He had thought about that. He needed local law enforcement to be more involved, but he also didn't know them anymore.

She pointed at him. "You have a trust issue."

He chuckled. "You could say that."

"I'm not saying I blame you. I feel the same way, but

I don't know any of the people from Cedar Hollow. You do. We have to trust someone."

"I trust my family. And the sheriff..."

"But..."

Ever since Giselle was shot, he got the feeling some of the deputies, and yes, maybe even Sheriff Copeland didn't have faith in his abilities as a law officer any longer. Cash told him it was in his head, but he still wondered. Even though Clive was no longer part of the department, he didn't need anyone at his side doubting his abilities or second-guessing him. But she was right. "I will call the sheriff."

Holly waited while he called. When the sheriff answered, Clive said, "I need your assistance."

"What is it? Have you learned something more on the gunmen? If you have, you're obligated to let my department know."

Clive didn't like the reprimand, but he shoved it aside. He quickly explained about the text sent to Holly.

"It doesn't sound that serious, but I would rather make certain it is not a setup. Have you thought of calling Dixie to simply check?"

"I have." He took a deep breath. It was a sensible question. "But if I call her and she's not the one who texted Holly, then Dixie may tip someone else off unknowingly about the meeting."

The sheriff quickly retorted, "You certain you're not being a tad paranoid, Clive?"

Clive refrained from sighing or showing his frustration even though inwardly it was eating him up. "The area code is from south Texas. There's more than the two men who killed the Mitchells that have attacked Holly. I don't want to take any chances. I don't think that is being paranoid."

He was met with a couple of seconds of silence, before the lawman said, "I hear you. I'll send Deputy Woods to meet you at the feed store."

"Thanks." He wanted the backup because an extra gun could come in handy since Clive didn't know what they might be walking into. But he wished it was one of his brothers meeting him. Deputy Woods was new to the department, and Clive didn't know much about him.

"I'm going," she reiterated.

He was afraid if Holly didn't show up at the feed store, the texter would leave, and they'd be no closer apprehending these guys. "Okay. We're in desperate need of answers, and it's important we don't make any mistakes. We need a foolproof plan."

This felt like the first good opportunity they had to learn about who was targeting them besides the hit men. He would have to be prepared for anything because he had the feeling this was a setup. How the person planned to carry it out, he had no idea.

TEN

While parked behind the Greasy Griddle for the past eleven minutes, Holly had been waiting to hear back from Clive. He had told her not to go to the feed store until he had contacted her, telling her he was in place. Time crawled by. Every little noise had her jumping. There were no cars parked at the diner, which meant everyone had gone home before she had arrived.

Headlights reflected on the street. As the vehicle approached, she automatically sank lower into the seat. The car halted at the stop sign down the street, with its turn signal blinking. The car turned right before disappearing up the block.

A breath whooshed from her lungs. She would be glad to get this meeting over with. It would be a relief if Dixie showed up at the feed store and had papers for her to sign so she could move into her house. It was only two more days until her move-in date, but it felt like forever before Monday would get here. A small part of her hoped the person behind the attacks was there so the man or people could be caught. But not really. She didn't know what she wanted.

Please keep me and the baby safe tonight, Lord. No matter what happens.

Her cell phone dinged, making her jump.

Deputy Woods is here and we're in place. The lights are on in the store.

She shifted Clive's pickup into Drive and pulled onto the road. Griffin's Farm and Feed was only four blocks away, and her apprehension grew as she drove closer. According to their plan, Clive and the deputy were supposed to meet two blocks away at Blaire's Chic Cuts and then walk to the feed store. Holly's instructions were to park in the front and come through the door where the lighting was best.

If Dixie was the one who set up the meeting, then it was presumed that the lights would be on inside. A dim light shone through the window. Holly climbed out of her vehicle, wishing she had a gun or something to protect herself. Clive had asked her, but she admitted she'd never fired one. A cold gust hit, sending chills straight through her.

She pulled the metal handle, and the door opened. Her heart hammered in her chest as she called out, "I'm here."

There was no answer.

She'd never been in the store before, and it took a moment to survey the room as she took another step inside. Six aisles stocked with a variety of goods took up the center of the store. A glass refrigerator stood at the end of the first aisle, which looked like it contained a variety of pet and livestock medications. Multiple pallets of feed were stacked along the back of the room. A Restroom sign stood above an open doorway to a lit hallway.

"Hello. Dixie? Are you here?" She took a few more steps inside while listening for movement but hearing nothing. Where was Clive and the deputy? Could they see her?

A foot scraped on the concrete floor.

She jerked around to look at the back of the room. A mirror hung from the ceiling in the far corner by the end of the last aisle and reflected down on a person dressed in dark clothing, hunched forward and inching down the aisle. She couldn't tell if he carried a weapon or not.

This wasn't Dixie. Holly quickly moved to the closet shelves, careful to stay low and out of view of the person. When she got to the end, she carefully peeked at the mirror. The man was gone. Her heart hammered in her chest. Where was he?

Clive had promised he would be watching, but she had the desire to run out the front door to the truck. At least then she could flee. If she didn't get shot first...

An unfamiliar man's voice called, "Where did you go?"

Holly hunkered down beside the shelf of dog leashes and collars. Clive had told her to stay put, but it was difficult considering she wanted to bolt. If she could just make it back to the vehicle, she would be gone. But he had asked her not to do that, and she didn't want to make things worse.

Footsteps softly sounded on the floor as the person neared the end of her aisle. The shelves backed up to the wall, giving her no escape route. Clive had told her if she felt safe, to talk with the person who had set up the meeting. The man walked out in the open. His hands were empty, but that didn't mean he didn't have a gun. "Holly. Are you here? My mom asked me to have you sign the rental agreement."

For just a second, doubt clouded her resolve. Was it

possible Dixie's son had been asked to get the papers signed? If so, she was going to feel foolish for making a big deal out of nothing. Still.

The man's gaze landed on her, and he chuckled. "What are you doing in the corner?"

In her peripheral vision, she saw Clive move into position behind one of the pallets of dog food, but she did not see the deputy. She hoped Clive or the deputy would not just shoot the man but hopefully try to arrest him if possible. Even though she had grown up in rough neighborhoods, she had never seen this much violence, especially in only a couple of days. She had her fill and didn't want to witness any more. And she sure didn't want her baby to witness this kind of danger on a regular basis.

She just wanted to make sure she was not in the line of fire and remained against the wall. "I called out when I came in, but no one answered. Was it you who texted me? I had been talking with Dixie about the rental."

"I'm Jake Griffin, Dixie's son."

As the man moved into the light from the hallway, she noticed his white running shoes. He was medium built much like the man who'd been in her hospital room. Clive had told her if it was someone besides Dixie, to try to learn what the person wanted, but only if it was safe. "You said I needed to sign papers. I'd been under the impression when I agreed to the conditions in the email that made our agreement complete. I need a place to live, so I'll sign whatever is required as long as the conditions remain the same."

The man glanced around the room like he was looking for someone. "I'm surprised you didn't bring Cantrell with you. If you're going to stay in Cedar Hollow you might want to consider making better friends. Clive can't be trusted to keep you safe. Don't know if you're aware, but he allowed his pregnant wife to be shot. Giselle lost the baby, and it ruined her. I'd hate to see that happen to you."

Holly swallowed hard. For this man to make light of Clive's unfortunate past was incredibly mean. It brought back memories of all the times others had said cruel things to her when she was the new kid in town. "I can pick my own friends."

"I'm sure you can." He walked over and flipped up the main light switch, fully illuminating the room. "But don't say I didn't warn you. Word around town is he was forced to quit the sheriff's department. Even in his family's security business, the brothers prefer him to spend his time working on the ranch or only allow him to investigate cases. He's never in charge of protecting a client."

She was careful not to glance in Clive's direction to give his position away. Jake's talk was going nowhere. "Is this what you really called me down here for? I thought you had papers for me to sign. I need to be going."

The man took a step closer, and his gaze darkened. "You're in danger and Cantrell can't protect you from—"

"Hold it right there." Clive's voice carried across the open room.

The man froze.

"Drop your weapon that's in your pocket." Clive's command was simple.

Please, Lord, let this be over now. Let Jake do as he was asked.

Jake's head jerked before his hands went into the air. "Don't shoot."

Holly slightly relaxed.

Clive took a step out from the stack of dog food bags

when all of a sudden, the front glass window exploded. Jake fell to the floor.

Holly dropped to her hands and knees to the concrete. Where had that come from?

A deputy ran into the room through the back door with his gun drawn. "Where did that shot come from?"

"Out front." Clive hit the light switch, plunging the room into darkness. "Stay put, Holly."

Clive hurried across the floor, careful to stick to the shadows. He dropped to one knee and checked Jake for a pulse. His phone lit up, and she realized he must be calling the paramedics.

The deputy went out of the front door, but instead of sticking to the shadows, he was out in the open.

"Stay with Jake until help arrives," Clive told Holly. "He doesn't appear to have any more weapons on him."

"Be careful," she told Clive as he hurried out the front door.

Jake lay on the floor, his face scrunched up as if he was in pain. He kicked his foot and groaned.

She moved to the end of the aisle but still stayed behind the shelves just in case he wasn't injured like he appeared to be. "Help is on the way."

Jake didn't respond to her words, and she wasn't even certain he heard her. Several minutes passed before Clive came back inside just as sirens wailed up the street. "Has he said anything more?"

She shook her head no. "Just groaning. He seems to be in a lot of pain."

"I'm sure he is." There was no empathy in Clive's voice. Not that she could blame him.

Two paramedics came through the door with a stretcher, and Holly stepped out of the way. She couldn't believe there had been another shooting. When would this stop? And the big question was, why had someone shot Jake Griffin? Had it been a case of mistaken identity, and the shooter believed it was Clive?

It took over thirty minutes for the paramedics to get Jake stabilized and moved to the ambulance. During that time, two more deputies arrived to help process the scene. Deputy Scott Jenkins was the one who took their statements and seemed to be the lead investigator. Clive turned around to look for Deputy Woods, but he had stepped out.

They had already interviewed Holly, and she sat behind the cash register counter on a stool, out of the way. He wished he knew what she was thinking for she seemed to be taking everything in. The dark circles under her eyes and slumped shoulders concerned him. The stress and running on no sleep wasn't good for her.

Was she thinking about Jake's words? Did she believe him that Clive had let his wife down? And that he wasn't good at his job? The man's comments more than irked him. Jake had worked for the feed store ever since he was a teenager in his parents' business. A few years ago, they began to trust him with more of the duties. Even as a teenager he'd been the one to deliver supplies to the ranch when needed. Most of the time, one of the ranch hands or Clive himself went into town to buy goods, but occasionally the list was too long, and the feed store always made deliveries free of charge with a minimum order.

What bothered Clive more was Jake's animosity toward him. Where had that come from? Jake had always been professional and as friendly as anyone else. He used to come by the ranch and stay to visit for a while when he made deliveries.

"That about wraps it up here," Deputy Jenkins said. "We may have more questions later the more we delve into this. But you know that already. Paul and Dixie should be here any minute."

The worst part of the job was informing kinfolks when a tragedy happened. Hopefully, Jake would pull through. Not just for their sake, but to get some answers, too. "Jenkins, do any suspects of who might have shot Jake come to mind?"

The older deputy shook his head. "Not so far."

Clive was afraid of that. "It doesn't make much sense. Unless Jake was involved in the killing of the Mitchells. Have you ever known him to be involved in drugs or in this kind of violence?"

The deputy's expression was serious. "No. Jake's record is clean except for a couple of speeding tickets. He comes from a good family."

"Yes, he does." Clive walked over to Holly. He hoped she didn't believe everything Jake had said about him not being good at his job. Would she doubt him even more? "We should be free to go now."

"Go where?" she said with a shrug. "You may know all of these people, but they're all strangers to me. I don't understand the connections."

"Me either, but we will. You can count on that."

She nodded but didn't reply.

Great. She probably didn't believe he could be counted on. His throat grew tight. He intended to prove her wrong, and many in the county, including his family.

They walked to his truck, and he climbed in on the driver's side. "It's late. You must be exhausted."

"I am. I can't even think straight." She glanced his

way. "Do you think Dixie will renege on letting me rent the house after this?"

"I wouldn't think so. I don't know what's going on with Jake or what he's involved in, but I do not think his parents are a part of it."

"Where to?" Holly asked.

"Back to the ranch for now." It was well past midnight, and they were just running on fumes. "You can turn off your cell now. I figure anyone might guess where we're going, but I don't want to broadcast if someone is tracking your phone."

He hoped it wasn't a mistake going back to the ranch. Right now, it didn't seem to matter where they were or who was around. The attacks just kept coming. They arrived back at the ranch house without trouble. Mollie Beth met him at his truck with her tail wagging. He rubbed her on the head and patted her side. "Hello, girl. You should be in bed by now."

Holly joined him in loving on the dog. "She's such a sweetheart. I miss having a dog."

He glanced at her. "You grew up with animals?"

"Not really. My dad and I moved around too much. But my Aunt Camilla had a beagle mix, and he became my best friend."

They went into the house, and this time he allowed Mollie Beth to come in since it was cold outside. She had been outside the night Holly was attacked, and it didn't prevent someone getting into their house. Which bugged him. She was an easygoing dog and had been upset the night Holly was tossed out the window. But would she have attacked a stranger? He didn't know.

Holly started up the stairs when she stopped and put her hand to her belly.

"What is it? Are you okay?" he asked.

She smiled. "That kick was a good one. Feel this." Without asking, she took his hand and placed it on the side of her stomach. A movement fluttered under his hand, followed by an unmistakable kick.

Their eyes connected. He grinned. "I felt it." The sudden realization that he was getting too close to her caused him to break the touch. "Good night."

After he made sure Holly had settled in and Mollie Beth was lying on her bed in the living room, he went back out to check the premises. He did not see Owen or the other two hands. Of course being late, he had not called his foreman to let him know he and Holly were back on the ranch.

He checked the security cameras when he walked back into the office and noticed they all seemed to be working. At least Owen had taken care of that assignment.

Once he made certain everyone was safe and in bed, he made his way behind the barn to the quaint cabin. His parents had it built for him when he married Giselle. They had wanted him close to the main house, but knew he and his wife would need their privacy. It had only been lived in for a little over two years and sat empty longer than that after Giselle left him. He opened the door and walked in; the smell of cedar still lingered in the rooms. He had no desire to relive his and Giselle's failed marriage, but there was something about the animosity in Jake's tone that made him wonder if there was more to his wife leaving him than the shooting. He stepped into the back bedroom.

How could he have gotten himself in this situation again? He thought back to the day that Giselle was shot. If he could just have a do-over. Any warning that she was about to be targeted and shot. Of course, the guy hadn't really been after his wife. He had been trying to shoot Clive. The screeching tires, the startled look on Giselle's face, and then the loud pops. All followed by terrible pain in his thigh as he saw his wife go down on the sidewalk.

He and Giselle had not been getting along as it was. They had just gotten into a fight the night before about his job. She had wanted him to find another line of work and move to another area. Preferably in a city like Austin. He had argued, telling her she worried too much. He had been with the sheriff's department for seven years and none of the deputies had been killed or seriously injured during that time. Every job presented its risk, but he didn't believe it was riskier than working on the ranch or a construction job. She had known what he did for a living when she married him. Or at least that had been his defense the night before.

He still bore the scar of the shot he had taken by covering her body with his after the first shot sounded. He had even believed that he had managed to protect her until he saw the blood on her. Confused, and believing it was his own blood that had been transferred to her, his immediate response was relief as soon as the shooter went down.

He walked over to the stuffed elephant that sat on the dresser. It had gone unused. Untouched. Deep down he was afraid to get too attached to Holly, or the thought of her baby for fear of losing everything again. Feeling the baby move made it all too real for him. He remembered reading the Scripture as a child about John the Baptist sleeping in his mother's womb before he was ever born. It seemed like that verse meant more to him now than it ever had before.

Holly was counting on him. But he didn't even know

where to start or who the men were who were targeting her. Yes, she had just witnessed a murder. It still bothered him that he didn't know the identity or recognize the older hit man, nor did he know who shot Jake. Unless the older hitman was the one to shoot Jake, that meant there were at least three people involved in the killings. Much bigger than what Cedar Hollow or the surrounding areas normally saw in crime.

His phone dinged, and he answered it on the first ring. "What do you have for me?"

Hawk said, "I'm not having any success with Deputy Woods. So far, he has come back clean, but I'll keep digging. I've been researching databases on drug deals and possible dealers in the area. Most of them have been around for years, and you would be familiar with them—José Rodriguez, Jeremy Meadows, Richard Gray. And a few other small players. Nothing so far and none that I would believe would hire a hit on the Mitchells or actively come after Holly and you. This doesn't have any of those guys' name on it that I can tell. Sorry, brother."

"Keep digging to see if Deputy Woods has let any of the guys off the hook or failed to investigate. We've got to be missing something."

"I'll try, but you know that's going to be difficult information to obtain."

"I know. It could be an out-of-town deal." Clive considered that for a moment. What if he was wrong? Occasionally people from out of town did come into the area to sell their drugs or to get away from law enforcement in some other part of the state or the country. Being that there were a lot of wooded areas and lakes, it made for a great hideout. Or so many thought. But what if it was someone from the area?

There was always a chance someone from the outside hired locals. Clive didn't get around as much as he used to when he was a deputy, but he still had contacts within the department. A couple of guys, plus the sheriff who would share information if he asked. "I don't know," he told Hawk. "I understand Holly being in trouble for witnessing a murder, but I question if the man who attacked her at the ranch knew the area."

"As in had been to the ranch before?"

"Yeah. It seemed a little too easy for him to get inside the house undetected and past Mollie Beth."

There was a pause on the phone before his brother said, "We will figure this out."

"I hope you're right."

After they disconnected Clive considered the situation as he walked back to the main house and then went into the living room. Maybe that's what was bothering him so much. He was afraid it was someone local or maybe even someone he knew who was behind the attacks.

"Are you busy?" He glanced up to see Holly standing there, her hair dangling past her shoulders. Even dressed in a pair of yoga pants and a large sweatshirt, she looked cute to him. Bags had formed under her eyes, telling him she had missed too much sleep. "Come on in. I just got off the phone."

She sat down on the couch across from him and folded her legs underneath herself. On the bottom of her socks were the words I'd Rather Be Baking. A large chocolate cupcake and frosting formed the toes. "I can't sleep. I'm worried about the private investigator who was following me. I don't want my ex-mother-in-law to cause trouble, but I'm afraid that's just what's going to happen."

"You have killers chasing you, and it's your mother-in-law who has you awake?"

"I'm concerned about everything," she said with an attitude. "My mother-in-law. Jake Griffin. The man I saw kill Sabrina Mitchell. I can't get the image out of my head. I'm afraid one wrong move, one moment when I relax and walk outside, or get into a vehicle, that the older man will simply squeeze a trigger, and it will all be over. If not, and I survive their attempts, then Margot will convince a judge my baby's life is in danger, and he will grant her custody."

He got up and moved beside her on the couch. He pulled her hands into his. "Go to bed and get some sleep. I'm not going to let any of that happen to you."

Her lip twitched like she doubted his words. "I don't know how you will stop it, but I'm glad you're standing beside me."

He grabbed a blanket and positioned himself in the leather recliner in the living room, which was located in the middle of the house. If anyone was going to make it upstairs to Holly, they would have to get by him and Mollie Beth first.

Before he drifted off to sleep, thoughts of Jake Griffin continued to bombard him. Who shot him and why? He had been a surprise piece of the puzzle. Had he been the one behind everything? Clive didn't see how, but he intended to make a trip back to the feed store early in the morning.

He would be getting answers if it was the last thing he did.

ELEVEN

Holly awoke the next morning before it was daylight. When she tried to sit up, her back and neck were sore. She knew she slept hard, but she must not have rolled over the entire night. She got up and quickly showered and put on clean clothes before going downstairs.

Even before she made it to the kitchen, a delicious aroma hit her. A pan of homemade biscuits sat on the stovetop, with a stick of butter and two jars of jam beside it.

"Help yourself to some," Shaylee said, walking into the room.

"These look delicious. Just like my grandma used to make. I never realized how blessed I was as a kid growing up and eating her cooking until she was gone." Holly smeared a healthy dose of butter and strawberry jam on two biscuits.

"I'm not good at making a lot of things, but Nora, the matriarch of the family, showed me their family recipe." Shaylee sat at the counter on a barstool decorated with a large metal star.

Holly joined her, and she started to dig in when she remembered to say grace. Normally she would say the blessing to herself, but it felt wrong with Shaylee sitting there so she said it out loud. The cook must be used to it because she didn't look awkward or surprised.

Shaylee asked, "Y'all were out late last night. I was worried when I heard you come in after two. Is everything okay?"

Holly used a paper napkin to dab the butter from the edge of her lips. "Again, these are absolutely delicious. I will want your recipe. Can I ask how you knew it was us last night who came in and not an intruder?"

She smiled. "The security cameras are connected to our phones. I didn't used to be on that list, but Clive added me after you were attacked."

"I didn't realize that. To answer your question, it was pretty nerve-racking last night." She went on to explain about the mysterious text and then about meeting Jake at the feed store and him being shot.

Shaylee shook her head. "I can't believe it. Why would someone shoot Jake?"

"You know him well?"

"I wouldn't say that exactly. But he's made deliveries to the ranch. He has always been friendly and sometimes even talkative when he comes by. Always asking how everyone is doing and the animals. That type of thing."

"What about Clive? Did he like him?" Holly still found it strange that Jake had tried to warn her about him.

Shaylee shrugged. "I guess so. He's never had anything bad to say about him, and occasionally, I see them visit whenever he comes by. Why? Did something happen?"

Holly didn't know how much to say. No doubt it was infuriating, and probably hurtful for Clive to hear Jake's words. She didn't want to overstep her bounds. "Jake warned me not to trust Clive to protect me. That he wasn't able to protect his pregnant wife. It wasn't just that he said it, but like he blamed Clive."

Shaylee's gaze went behind Holly's head.

"I can keep you safe." Clive's voice came out clipped.

Holly's hand went to her chest. "I'm sorry. I did not hear you come in. I didn't mean anything—"

He held the palm of his hand in the air, telling her to stop. "I'm going to the feed store this morning and Paul Griffin is meeting me there. You're welcome to go with me. Unless you don't believe I can keep you safe."

Holly got to her feet. Even though she understood the jab, it hurt more than it should have. "Clive, I trust you." To her surprise, the words were true.

"I'll be ready to go in five minutes." He grabbed a couple biscuits from the pan and held one in the air. "Thank you, Shaylee." With that he walked out of the room, and Holly heard him disappear upstairs.

Two men walked through the back door without knocking. The older one said, "Clive said we could have some biscuits."

"Help yourselves." Shaylee smiled. "Holly, have you met Sammy and Utah?"

She shook her head no.

Shaylee introduced the older man as Sammy and the younger one as Utah.

Holly said, "Glad to meet you."

They filled their hands without bothering with a plate. Sammy looked at Holly. "We've heard what has been going on. Just to let you know, we'll keep an eye out on the ranch for any trouble."

Utah nodded. "Yeah."

"Thank you both. I hope we don't have any more trouble." Holly watched them leave with their hands full.

Shaylee said in a quiet voice, "Don't worry about Clive overhearing."

Holly sighed inwardly. "It's got to eat him up that his wife was shot with him standing right there, but he shouldn't blame himself. I doubt he could have prevented it."

"You're right. He dived in front of her to try to protect her and took a bullet. But it wasn't enough."

"He took a bullet?"

Shaylee glanced over her shoulder toward where Clive had disappeared before answering. "In the thigh. The injury still bothers him sometimes, but he would never admit it."

As Clive came back down the stairs, Holly's heart went out to him. The cowboy had so many secrets, but she wished he would open up to her more. It was clear this situation was nothing but an arrangement where he felt he was doing his duty.

When Clive walked back into the kitchen, he got the feeling they had been talking about him. He couldn't worry about that now. He needed answers. Tonight, his family would be home, and he hoped he had progress to report. "Let's go."

He caught Holly and Shaylee exchanging glances before Holly followed him out the door. He wasn't in the mood for talk and was glad she must have felt the same on the ride over. It wasn't until they were on the edge of Cedar Hollow that she asked, "Is there anything in particular you're hoping to find?"

"Not really. Anything."

"Don't be irritated. I shouldn't have been telling Shaylee

what Jake said, but she asked what happened. I'm sorry. I shouldn't have said anything."

"It's not a big deal." Clive still didn't understand why Jake had said those things, almost like they were enemies. It's not like they had been close friends, but they had always been cordial. "I never realized Jake didn't like me, so it caught me by surprise."

"Yeah, it sounded like he didn't like you. I don't see how."

Clive didn't respond to her summing up the situation. He pulled into the parking lot, praying they would learn something helpful. Normally, the store would be open at seven, but the Closed sign was still on, and yellow crime scene tape was over the door.

When he walked to the front door, Paul must've seen him coming because he unlocked the door and let them in. "Thank you for letting us come by."

The front half of the room was marked off by more of the yellow tape.

The older man frowned. "I hope you can give me some answers. The deputies and Sheriff Copeland couldn't tell us much except they believe it was a drive-by shooting. Deputy Jenkins told me I could come by the store, but I wasn't to touch anything. He said he thought they had gathered all the evidence. You were here last night?"

"Yeah, I was. Holly—" Clive indicated her with his hand as an introduction, "—received a message that she needed to sign papers for the house Dixie is renting to her on Monday. She was asked to meet her at the feed store."

"I wasn't aware Dixie was meeting with anyone. She was home last night. They're starting a new show where they're converting old barns and grain silos into homes. Dixie had been talking about it all week. One of the homes was from West Texas near Muleshoe where she grew up. She was hoping to recognize the silo."

"Here."

Clive turned to see Holly as she pulled out her cell phone and showed Paul the message.

Paul squinted at the phone. "That's not our number. Did you tell Jake you were coming by? Is that why he was here?"

"We didn't tell anyone except for the sheriff. Holly didn't get the message until late." Clive looked back at the street. A bullet hole had fractured the glass. People were out and about in town. "Let's get away from this window."

They all moved to the center of the room.

"That's not Jake's number either unless he got a new number but didn't tell us."

"Do you mind if I look out back?" Clive was ready to search the place, hoping to find something the investigators missed. And maybe he wanted to check what Jake had been up to since his behavior last night had him baffled.

Paul shook his head. "Go ahead. The deputies were here until late last night. They didn't say anything about searching the warehouse."

"You know I'm not with law enforcement anymore, but the shooting has me wondering why someone shot your son. We won't disturb anything." He motioned for Holly to follow him out the back door.

Paul followed him, too. "Dixie is beside herself waiting for Jake to tell us what happened. They have him sedated right now and preparing him for surgery."

"I'm sorry. It's got to be agonizing for her. I'm working with the sheriff and hope we have answers soon." Clive didn't blame the man, but he would have preferred to look around without having to carry on a conversation.

He didn't even know what he was looking for, but he wondered if Jake was tied to the two hit men who killed the Mitchells. It was too much of a coincidence for the two crimes not to be connected.

Holly told Paul, "If you need another day or two before I can move into the house, I understand."

"Naw. I don't think that's necessary."

Clive was glad for Holly conversing with Paul so he could concentrate on seeing if he could learn why someone targeted the store owner. On the far wall of the open warehouse-type room, there was a cluttered desk with heaps of paper. Multiple boxes were piled around, making getting around the desk like going through a maze. Stacks of receipts appeared to have fallen on top of each other. A cork board hung on the wall behind the desk with a calendar that was on March of last year.

If he hoped to find a connection between Jake and the Mitchells, he didn't expect to find a receipt for drugs sold, but he quickly sifted through a couple of stacks of papers on the desk. Most of them were from delivery receipts of feed and supplies. A few were of utility bills and overdue notices. Accounting at the store must be a nightmare and probably incorrect. It made him wonder if Jake even filed taxes, or maybe he just made up the amount of income and expenses.

So far, he hadn't found anything incriminating, but it would take a week to go through all the paperwork. There simply was no time for that. He continued to scout around looking everything over, hoping something would jump out at him. He might have to wait until Jake came out of surgery to interview him.

If Jake would even talk with him. If Jake knew who

shot him, he might be more than willing to talk if he thought it would keep him safe.

A broom leaned against the wall in the corner, and a pile of dirt and trash lay in front of it. A fifty-five-gallon plastic barrel sat beside it with trash overflowing. When he glanced at the dirt pile, he noticed a crumbled foil pack laying among debris. Careful not to touch it, he turned it over with a pen he had in his pocket. OxyContin 80 mg.

He didn't know Jake had any kind of health issue that would require such a dose of pain relief, but he did know fentanyl was disguised as other pills. He wondered if he could get these tested. If it was fentanyl, he may have just found his first connection.

Knowing he'd need the sheriff's department, he pulled out his burner phone to call Sheriff Copeland. He stepped on a discarded PVC pipe and lost his balance, making him bump into the broom. The handle hit the bulletin board and knocked it to the ground. When he bent to retrieve it, a photo fluttered to the floor. He grabbed it and turned it over.

It was a picture of Giselle.

She wore a big smile and held her hand under her chin like she was posing in a flirty way. Clive recognized the blue dress she was wearing instantly. It had been a birthday present from him the summer she told him she was pregnant.

What was Jake doing with a picture of his ex-wife?

His stomach tightened into a hard knot as a sinking feeling descended on him. The shot was zoomed in on Giselle, but he could still make out the wooden wall in the background. This was taken in his barn in front of one of the stalls. His fingers tightened into a ball, crinkling the photo.

"Did you find anything helpful?"

He glanced up, and Holly stopped in her tracks.

"Mr. Griffin got a phone call... Are you alright?"

Not one bit. "I found an OxyContin pill package. We can have it tested. If it's fentanyl, we may have a connection to the Mitchells, but we need to move fast. If Jake is behind this, I want him prosecuted to the highest extent of the law."

Holly's gaze fell to the photo in his grasp, and she cocked her head to the side. "Who is that?"

A lump formed in his throat and refused to dislodge. The thought that his wife may have cheated on him with Jake had humiliation pounding him like a violent hailstorm. He didn't want to answer Holly, but he knew this was too important to keep secret. "It's Giselle."

"Your wife?" She did a double take at the photo, seemingly taking it in. Then she shook her head. "I don't know what to say."

Her comforting tone was mildly annoying, even though she probably meant well. He didn't need to be coddled. "I'm going to get to the bottom of this. No matter who's involved or what I learn. I will keep digging until I find the truth or die trying."

TWELVE

Holly knew there was nothing she could say to Clive to ease the pain he was going through. He was a rugged cowboy, but even tough guys didn't like to suspect their ex-wife may have been cheating while they were still married. She stepped back to give him some room.

Paul Griffin walked over to Clive. "Did you find anything that will tell us who shot Jake?"

Instead of answering, he asked, "Did your son have any medical conditions that caused him to be on pain medication?"

Paul frowned and shook his head. "Not that I know of."

"Okay. Did he speak much of Giselle?"

"Giselle?" The older man eyebrows drew in like he was confused "Your wife? Uh, sorry, ex-wife. No, Jake didn't. Why?"

Clive shifted his weight to his other foot. "He had a photo of her on his bulletin board. I hadn't realized they were that close. I think that's all I need for now." He motioned for Holly to follow.

They walked out of the warehouse as Mr. Giffin hollered, "Let me know if you learn anything."

Clive called over his shoulder, "I will."

As they settled in his truck, she turned to him. "That was awkward."

"I know it. But if Jake was into drugs, the person who shot him could've been the older hit man. I need to know who's calling the shots. I'm hoping we can learn the identity of the younger man killed at the vacation home. We need to pay Sheriff Copeland a visit."

Holly thought he was finished, when Clive added quietly, "And we need to learn what this has to do with my ex."

She asked, "How far is it to the sheriff's department?"

"About three miles outside of town."

Clive was probably not in the mood for conversation, so she stared out her passenger-side window. How did Jake connect to the Mitchells? Drugs had to be the answer, which would mean the store owner was involved. As a buyer or seller? Holly didn't know him, but he had to be in deep for someone to shoot him. Where did Clive's ex-wife fit in?

Even though she'd lived with her Aunt Camilla, and things hadn't been great, Holly had thankfully never gotten involved in drugs or alcohol. She had been used to making decisions on her own. Her own calls. Good or bad.

Grandma Harvey—her dad's mom—had told her to think about her actions. She had been a good influence on Holly and had taught her to love baking. Grandma lived in the country on a small farm. She was concerned about her granddaughter getting hurt and didn't allow her to do a lot of things that Holly wanted to do, but she had always known her grandmother loved her. Holly thought it was because she didn't have a mom in her life. And even though Holly loved her daddy, and he had cared about her, she knew he'd not been the best influence on her. She had been left alone at a young age to fend for herself. Most of the time, he was home by 7:00 or 8:00 p.m. from work, but sometimes it was much later than that. Most parents did not leave a ten-year-old child home by themselves at that time of night. Holly knew this from the other kids at school and occasionally when she moved to a new town some other parent would take notice and would invite her to come over and eat supper with them.

But her daddy always said no since they could make it on their own. This was probably why she was relieved when Alec had taken notice of her and wanted to do things for her. *Spoil her* was how he'd put it. She had welcomed the attention. Alec had made all their decisions, from financial, to what she did during the day, to what they did for fun. It might not have been such a bad thing, except Holly didn't even know what she wanted to do. She had lost herself. Her identity and her backbone. She had even considered it a challenge to gain her mother-in-law's approval and had accepted it with vigor.

Little did she know, there was zero chance to impress the woman.

When things began to spin out of control with Alec, the baby had brought Holly hope. In the end, it was the catalyst that drove her husband over the edge. So as Holly had done ever since her husband's funeral, she turned to God. She wished that she had been brought to church her whole childhood because things might have turned out different for her. Her grandma had brought her to services when she spent the summers with her, and Holly was a firm believer that it was never too late to make changes, positive changes. She bowed her head and talked to God.

Even though they must be getting close to the sheriff's department, she closed her eyes. *Please, Lord, help us to figure out who the hit men are and who shot Jake. Be with the doctors so Jake can recover. I don't know him, but no one should be shot down like that. Please, be with Clive. Help him to find the answers we're looking for and that he will handle the truth no matter what it is. And keep us safe. Amen.*

"We're here." Clive glanced at Holly and noticed her eyes had been closed. "Wake up."

She smiled. "I wasn't asleep."

He glanced at her again before they got out of his truck. It surprised him he was glad she was with him. Not just to keep her safe, but she had a calming effect on him too.

"Hold on." He hurried around to her side of the vehicle while she climbed out. He glanced around to make sure there were no suspicious vehicles approaching.

Satisfied it was safe, he walked her into the building and the dispatcher waved them back to the sheriff's office.

The sheriff looked up from his desk at both of them before he addressed Clive. "I need you to keep me abreast of the situation."

Clive detected annoyance in his tone and did not want to get on the man's bad side. He told him everything they'd learned, including the OxyContin and the photo Jake had of Giselle.

A glance at Holly showed her staring at the floor. He knew she was listening, but at least she had the grace not to act eager to hear all about it.

The sheriff leaned back in his chair and stared at him. "You need to leave this case to us."

Clive was no longer with the department but resisted saying the words. Technically, as long as he didn't impede the investigation, he wasn't breaking the law; they were on the same side.

"You need to let one of our investigators interview Jake."

If the sheriff expected him to argue, Clive wasn't going to oblige. He didn't want him to put one of the deputies in charge of protecting Holly. She had witnessed a murder, and the sheriff wouldn't request the US Marshals put her in witness protection unless he knew who was behind the hit. The situation was too dangerous not to have law enforcement behind him. "I won't go by the hospital to speak with him."

"You were a good deputy, Cantrell, but you remember how I conduct things. We go by the book, and Jake will be more forthcoming with one of my investigators if he had a thing going with your wife."

Clive swallowed the irritation in this throat. He doubted any of them could get as much information out of Jake as he could, but Clive wasn't certain how he'd respond if he learned Jake had an affair with his wife. Giselle had moved on and was married to someone else now, but the thought still rankled him. If she had an affair with Jake, were there others? Did everyone in town or anyone in Clive's family know? "Just keep me in the loop, Sheriff."

"That goes for you, too." He glanced at the clipboard on his desk. "I got a call from Murphy County Sheriff's Department. They learned the identification of the man you shot. Twenty-six-year-old Brodie Hoffman from Corpus Christi. Have you heard of him?"

"No, I haven't. Does he have a record?" Clive was relieved they had a name, and he prayed they had something that would lead to the other man.

"A short list. One possession of an illegal substance and a DWI. The possession charge of LSD from four years ago was dismissed because the prosecutor couldn't establish possession. The DWI from five years ago was his first offense, and he received a fine of $2000."

"So nothing recent. Either he doesn't do drugs anymore, or he learned how to not get caught."

The sheriff nodded. "My gut says the latter, but we don't know for certain. We'll keep digging."

"Thanks." He turned to Holly. "Ready?"

"Yeah."

As they got to their feet, the sheriff added, "Miss Myers, we're working around the clock on the case. We're going to get the guys involved."

"I appreciate it." After they walked out of the sheriff's office, Clive held the door open for her and they returned to his dually.

As soon as the door was shut, and he started the engine, she turned to him. "This still must be tough for you discussing your ex-wife. Things may not be as they appear."

"True." But seeing Giselle's smile for whoever was snapping the photo told him she enjoyed posing. Had his wife already planned on leaving him before the shooting? Maybe the incident had just hurried her decision to leave.

He couldn't afford to get sidetracked thinking about his failed relationship. He needed to know if Jake was the one who'd attacked Holly, and if he was connected to the hit men?

Clive had watched the deputies in the office. Most of them he recognized and had worked with. There were only a couple of new officers and only one or two that he didn't know.

Deputy Scott Jenkins pulled into the lot and parked beside Clive. Clive told Holly, "I'll be right back."

He hopped out of his truck and hurried over to Jenkins. He pointed at Deputy Woods who was standing at a printer in front of a window. Clive quietly asked, "Scott, what can you tell me about him?"

Jenkins looked over his shoulder. "That's Woods. He's been here seven or eight months."

It wasn't what Jenkins said, but his stoic body language as he said it. "I met him last night. What do you think of him?"

Jenkins rolled his head as if loosening his neck muscles. Then he moved closer and kept his voice low. "The jury is still out. But there's something about the man I don't care for." He started to say something more but then closed his mouth.

"What is it?"

The older man looked Clive straight in the eyes. "I didn't want to say anything until I was certain. Deputy Woods knew the victims. Or at least Tim Mitchell."

Clive didn't want to get his hopes up, but information was starting to come in and he didn't plan on slowing down until everyone involved was behind bars. Jenkins was old school and could be trusted. He didn't give information like this carelessly. "How do you know? Did you know Tim and Sabrina Mitchell?"

The older man shook his head. "Not really. I've seen them around town occasionally. Not much in Cedar Hollow but over by Wyndham Creek. Several months ago, I stopped in at the Burger Barn for something to eat after work. Woods was in a back booth visiting with someone, and I figured he was trying to unwind after a long day like me. Sometimes it's nice to get away from work and just leave it all behind. You know?"

Clive nodded. "Almost every day of my life when I worked for the department." That was no exaggeration.

"Deputy Woods was sitting with a man at the booth. They were deep in conversation. No big deal. Except when they were walking out, I heard Woods tell him to clean it up. I didn't think much about it until we started investigating the death of Tim and Sabrina Mitchell. I recognized Tim in the crime scene photos."

At least that gave Clive something to go on. "What do you figure they were talking about?"

"I don't know. But I was looking into it. I didn't plan to brief Sheriff Copeland until I knew more. You know how it goes."

Suspicion of another deputy tended to bring outsiders in since their department was too small to have Internal Affairs into it. And most law enforcement officers did not make that move until they were almost certain. "I understand."

"One thing I have noticed, Deputy Woods didn't mention his association with Tim Mitchell the other day when Copeland asked us during the briefing if any of us knew the man."

"There may not be anything here, but I'll discreetly look into it. Thank you, Scott."

"I want you to find out who killed those two people and shot Jake Griffin. If someone in the department has dirty hands, I want to know. Protect that young woman and mother-to-be."

"I plan on it." As Clive turned to leave, he glanced up and saw Sheriff Copeland watching them through the glass door. The man was savvy and would know that they were discussing the case. He was certain the sheriff would ask about it, but Clive intended to get his brothers looking deeper into the background of Deputy Woods. Even if the man wasn't guilty of anything, he must be holding back information. And the question was, why?

When he got back in his truck, he called Cash and explained the conversation he'd had with the sheriff and Deputy Jenkins. Cash agreed to take another look into Deputy Woods's background.

As they pulled away, Holly said, "It feels like things are starting to come together. I hope the deputy was not involved. Do you think he knows the older hit man? The one who carried the badge."

"Maybe. I already told Hawk about him so if there's a connection, he'll find it."

The more he considered the older hit man, the more he believed he could be connected to Deputy Woods. Or at least, it would make sense if the hit man was or had been in law enforcement. He agreed with Holly that everything felt like the information was starting to roll in. But he didn't have to remind himself that there were at least two men out there who'd attacked her—unless Jake was one of them. Even with progress, they didn't have solid answers.

He was afraid if Deputy Woods was involved, and he noticed Clive talking with the sheriff and Deputy Jenkins, Woods might be forced to move quickly.

Clive would be glad when his brothers were back because he had the feeling time was running out.

THIRTEEN

Holly would be glad to make it back to the ranch and rest. So much had been going on, and being pursued was just as mentally draining as it was physically. She prayed that if they could make it through the rest of the day and tonight without being attacked again, as soon as Clive's family was home, everything would be quickly solved.

But thirty minutes later when they pulled up to the ranch house, one of the ranch hands made a beeline out of the barn and straight to Clive's truck. Clive opened his door. "What is it, Utah?"

After glancing around to make certain no one else was about, Holly also climbed out so she could hear the conversation.

Utah looked over his shoulder before speaking quietly. "I don't know if I should say anything."

"Tell me what's going on and don't worry about anyone finding out."

Holly couldn't help but think that whatever Utah was about to say might have consequences.

"Okay." The ranch hand, who was a few years younger than her, swallowed and said, "Somebody in a black SUV was here."

Clive asked, "Tinted windows?"

Utah nodded. "I was in the barn watering the horses and Owen and Sammy went to town for another roll of barbwire. Shaylee was already gone when I got here, something about buying groceries. Owen said since I was late this morning I should stay here and finish the chores."

"Did you see the driver or talk to him?"

"No." He glanced down and kicked a rock with his boot. "I sorta hid behind the wall of the barn. Ever since Holly was tossed out of the window, I've been nervous. Sorry, boss."

Poor guy. Holly could tell it embarrassed him for not trying to confront the driver, but she didn't blame him.

"No need to apologize. What time was this?"

"About thirty minutes ago. But there's more. After the SUV left, a deputy drove by the ranch four times real slow. He didn't pull into the drive, but he stopped like he was looking for someone."

Clive clapped him on the shoulder. "You did good, Utah. Why don't you take the rest of the day off. Enjoy the weekend, and I'll see you on Monday."

The ranch hand's face lit up. "Really? Okay. You sure you don't need me?"

"I'm sure."

"I'll see you then."

After Utah hurried away, Clive turned to her. "I don't like this. I'm getting you to safety."

"We're not staying here?"

"Too many people about." He shook his head. "I trust Sheriff Copeland, but not so much his deputies, mainly Woods. My brothers will be home sometime tonight or in the morning at the latest. We're going to take cover at the line shack until my backup gets here. Get ready to ride."

"What about Shaylee?" She hated the thought of her being alone to fend for herself.

"I'm calling her right now." He quickly hit her number.

Holly listened as he asked her to turn around and stay at the Cedar Hollow Inn. He disconnected. "She'll be back at the ranch tomorrow."

"Good." Clive was probably right about not staying at the main house. And she didn't want to leave town again since that didn't stop someone from finding them. She quickly went inside the main house and layered her T-shirt with the flannel shirt. It was in the low fifties today, but the wind was mild. She grabbed an apple from the kitchen counter on the way out the door. Clive had his horse and the palomino saddled.

He looked like he was having second thoughts. "Are you good with riding in your condition?"

Grandma Harvey's constant warnings about being careful around horses played through her mind. Holly had ridden a few times every summer, but it wasn't like she had taken lessons. If she was thrown, the baby could be injured. The risk seemed lower than being met by a killer intent on eliminating her. "We have little choice."

He held a five-gallon bucket securely while she used it to step into the stirrup. Once she was seated, he asked, "Do you want a gun?"

"I've never shot one." She swallowed. "I'm not going to lie, they make me nervous."

"I could give you a quick lesson."

She shook her head. "No. I'm afraid I'd forget how to work it and shoot myself. Seriously."

He climbed into his saddle and looked at her. After a moment, he reached into his saddlebag and handed her a knife in a sheath. "Here. That's a Ka-Bar. It's sharp and can do damage. The only thing is you'd have to be close to your target."

She glanced at the knife before shoving it into her pants' side pocket. "Thanks. I just hope I don't need it."

As they rode out of the yard, Clive called Hawk and told him what was going on. After he'd explained what Utah had told him, he asked, "Did you get hold of Daniels?"

Clive listened, and Holly wished he had the call on speaker. After several minutes, he disconnected. "What is it?" she said.

He glanced at her. "Hawk finally got a hold of Hugh Daniels, which was easy. He's the guy that was in the sedan parked in the pasture by the Mitchell place. He's a private investigator. Margot Myers hired him to follow you."

Holly knew her mother-in-law had been involved, but she didn't reply because she wanted to hear the rest.

"Daniels denied having any connections to the hit men or the attacks on you. He'd been following you at a distance but then lost you on the outside of Cedar Hollow. By the time he found your car again, the house had already burned down, and investigators were working the scene. He stayed to see if you'd return."

Holly didn't know if she was relieved or not to hear that. "I don't know that I buy that story."

"Hawk either. That's why he called Margot."

"Really? What did she have to say?" For some reason it surprised Holly that they would go straight to the source, but she was glad Hawk had.

"She didn't deny hiring a PI to follow you. She claimed that after Alec died, she knew she wanted a relationship with his child. She claimed she doesn't want to hire a lawyer, but if she has to sue for grandparent's visitation rights then she will. Sorry. I'm sure that's not the news you wanted to hear."

The palomino, Duchess, had an easy gait and started up a long hill. "It's not. But I'll fight that battle later."

"We won't have good cell reception once we're over this hill."

"How far is the line shack?"

"It's not so much the distance, because it's about four miles the way the crow flies, but it'll take about two and half to three hours to get there because it's difficult to access. This is why I want us there. No one should be able to find us there, except for my family."

"I don't suppose there's any news on Jake?"

"You were there when I talked to the sheriff. I haven't heard anything since then."

Holly spent the next hour or so going back and forth between thinking about the case to thinking about her mother-in-law. She didn't blame a grandparent for wanting to be involved with their grandchild, but Holly didn't trust her. She felt betrayed by Alec, and she didn't trust his mother at all.

The wind started to pick up and the sky turned cloudy. She needed a break and hated to stop before they made it to the shack, but she couldn't put it off any longer. "I need a break."

"It's not much farther." Clive glanced over his shoulder at her.

She cocked her head at him and raised her eyebrows. "I *need* a break."

He held up his hand. "Okay. Sorry."

She pulled Duchess to a stop, and Clive waited to help her down. She was tempted to tell him she didn't need his assistance, but she honestly thought it was kind of sweet. Plus, she didn't want to accidently hang her foot in the stirrup or something and fall. Her pride was not that important.

While he held Duchess's reins, she hurried into the woods for about thirty yards and took care of business. She'd almost made it back to the trail when she didn't see a long tree root stretched across the path, tripping her. She fought to keep her balance, but failed, and went down to one knee. Even so, she managed to soften the impact.

She glanced up and her gaze fixed on a green box. She blinked. It looked like a camera—the kind hunters used to view animals in the area. Her dad had several of them through the years. She got back to her feet. "Hey. I found a camera."

He tied the horses to a bush and joined her.

She pointed at the camera. "I wouldn't have ever seen it if it weren't for me being eye to eye with it." She dusted off her knee.

Clive unstrapped the device from the pine tree before he opened it. He pulled out a SIM card. "I wonder who was putting out game cameras back here. If the SIM card is still good, hopefully, I'll be able to see who's been hunting back here."

"No one from the ranch hunts?"

"Occasionally. But not on our land." He stuck the card in his shirt pocket and put the camera in his saddle bag. "Let's get moving again. It won't be long before dark. I'll check this out later."

They both remounted. She was careful as she rode the palomino down the trail. There was no doubt if Clive was by himself, he would be moving at a much faster pace.

"There's a dip right there." The cowboy pointed to the ground to a low area so she wouldn't miss it.

It did her heart good to know that he was so protective of her. She also realized if there was another way to get back to this shack besides the horses, he would've never allowed her to ride. Twice he had told her to let him know if she was uncomfortable or if the ride was too much for her. But she was extremely aware of her condition and would do nothing to put the baby at risk.

He glanced over his shoulder. "The land has grown up in trees and brush more than I realized."

As silly as it was, riding horseback made her relax some. She felt so far away from town. It seemed impossible that anyone could find them back here. There was a chill in the air, and she was glad Clive had loaned her his heavy coat. The man appeared rough and sometimes too stern, but he had a soft side that appealed to her.

When they came to a barbwire gate, she waited while Clive opened it and then shut it behind her. The weather was crisp and overcast. When she lived near Dallas, she rarely spent time outside except when she visited Grandma Harvey. Everything felt so peaceful here. As soon as the thought crossed her mind, she almost laughed. She hadn't been free of danger from the moment she arrived in Cedar Hollow.

"What are you thinking?"

She smiled. "It's very serene here. I know we're riding to a shack, but I can't believe none of you have built your house in this area."

He chuckled. "It's a pretty sight all right. But you would have a hard time getting back here. The road would be so long that the expense wouldn't be worth it."

"You're right, it's just so lovely."

He nodded, and she noted the look of satisfaction on his face. She continued to follow his horse when it went into a draw. The ground was wet and muddy in some areas. The dead grass was tall. A rabbit darted out from the bushes and disappeared into the grass. Duchess merely twitched her ears but didn't startle by the sudden movement.

"Do the cows come back here?"

"Not anymore. It's too hard to get back here so we fenced it off at the gate we came through earlier. If a cow is calving or sick, you need to be able to check on it. It's close to our property's border so it's not like we're losing much grazing land."

A huge, long clearing stretched out in front of them. Clive put his hand in the air to stop her as he stared at the ground, his eyebrows drawn in a frown.

"What is it?"

"Tire tracks. No one should've been back here."

Holly could see the concern in his expression, and it made her stomach tense. "No one? What about the people who work on the ranch? Or your brothers?"

"I don't know how they made it back here. Years ago, when I was a kid there was a small bridge that went over Brush Creek. It was rarely used anyway but once it got too dilapidated to cross, we let it rot away. The only times we ever came back here was on horseback."

"What about the ATVs? Surely you could maneuver back here with one of those." She didn't know why she was asking these questions, for she surely did not have as much knowledge about the property as Clive did.

"It might be done. Obviously, someone managed it, but I don't know the route they took." He veered left and followed the path of the tracks, leaving Holly no choice but to follow suit. Clive continued, "I would like to know what someone was doing back here. If it was a ranch worker, he should've told us, which makes me believe it's someone from the outside."

Duchess picked up the pace to keep up. Clive's frown deepened, and she decided to quit asking questions even though her mind could not stop them from forming. Was it possible hunters had been on the land and used ATVs and simply did not ask permission? It's not like she knew anything about the ranch or pathways that were rarely used, but her dad occasionally went hunting on other people's land. She assumed her dad had permission, but she was just guessing. If there was a shack back here, she could only imagine that would make a good hunting lodge.

A long narrow meadow of short grass appeared in front of them. Clive pulled on the reins and stopped, surveying the whole area. After a moment, he swerved to the left and continued following the tire tracks. They had gone about fifty yards when something buzzed in the distance. At first, she couldn't tell what it was and thought it was a vehicle on some nearby road.

Something yellow in the sky caught her attention. A plane.

"Ride for the trees." Clive slapped his hand through the air, spun his horse around, then raced for the tree line.

Holly did the same, but Duchess was not interested in going fast. Holly gave her a kick in the sides with her tennis shoes. "Go. Come on Duchess." The horse picked up the pace a little but only made the bouncing up and down more uncomfortable. She urged her again with a nudge in the ribs. "Go."

Please, Lord, protect my baby.

The horse finally galloped, making her gait long and smooth. The buzz from the plane grew into a rumble right behind them. Holly didn't turn around but kept making for the safety of the trees.

A popping sounded over the rumble as bullets peppered the ground behind them.

Holly squealed.

Clive yanked on his reins, spinning the horse in the other direction, flying back toward her. He yelled as he passed her, "Keep going, Holly. Don't stop for anything."

More shots blasted but that sounded close like it must've come from Clive as he charged back in the plane's direction. Duchess made it to the edge of the trees just as three more shots boomed. Going against Clive's wishes, she pulled on the reins and looked back. Clive was on the ground, and his horse hoofed it across the airstrip. The plane was in a nosedive.

She gritted her teeth and held her breath as the plane crashed into the ground and exploded into a ball of flames.

Duchess whinnied and stomped her foot nervously. Holly patted her neck. "It's okay, girl. It's okay."

Tearing her gaze away from the fiery crash, she looked back at Clive, who was still lying on the ground. She nudged Duchess and the horse trotted toward the cowboy. Holly pulled on the reins to stop the palomino, then stepped out of the saddle and hurried to Clive's side. She knelt beside him and rubbed her thumb against his cheek. "Are you okay?" She didn't know what she would do if she lost him. That man had done everything in his power to keep her safe, and it might have cost him his life.

Clive's ears rang but a soft touch caressed his cheek. He opened his eyes to see Holly's beautiful eyes staring down at him, concern etched in her wrinkled forehead. "Clive, are you okay?"

He hurt all over, and when he tried to get to his feet his head pounded like a freight train had hit him. His hand went to the back of his head as he got to his feet. "I'm okay. I think. I wasn't shot." He might as well have taken a bullet for as bad as he felt. "When the guy shot right in front of me, it startled Binion, making him rear up." He turned to see the yellow Cessna in flames, and black smoke filled the sky. What was this guy doing here on his ranch? Whatever it was, it looked like he'd been using the airstrip for a while. If the pilot was to meet someone, the smoke could be seen for miles.

"Are you sure you weren't hit?" She held her arm out for him to take as if he needed assistance.

"I can walk." He whistled for Binion, but didn't see him. The horse might have started back for the corral. "I want you to stay away from the plane. There could be more explosions. Air fuel tends to be extremely explosive." As if on cue, another loud boom filled the air.

She flinched. "I'll go with you."

Walking beside Duchess and Holly, he continued for the tree line but also kept an eye on the plane and watched for any approaching vehicles.

"Why was that man shooting at us? And was it my imagination or was there at least two people on board?"

"There was." Every muscle in his back hurt, and his head was still throbbing. Binion had never tossed him before. Not that he could blame the horse, but he had still not expected it. As he watched the raging inferno in front of him, he realized someone must've been planning to meet the pilot, and they would be here soon. He didn't want Holly in the middle of this for surely there would be major trouble. "I need you to go to the line shack by yourself."

"I would rather wait on you. I can be patient."

"Holly, you don't understand. More trouble is headed our way, and we're miles from help. Those vehicle tracks tell me that someone's been coming back here to meet the plane. And they're probably not far behind. My Winchester is with Binion. We have no protection and will be sitting ducks."

Her face paled considerably. "But you don't even know what direction the people would be coming from. From the ranch or from a neighbor's property. Or they might be staying in the shack itself." He leaned his head back and looked up at the cloudy overcast sky. She was right. He couldn't send her to the shack unless he was certain it was secure. And he just had no idea what he would find.

"Then I want you to stay here in the trees and stay hidden. I'm going to check out the wreckage. If someone comes along, I want you to ride through the trees and then hightail it back to the ranch as fast as you can. Then call the sheriff."

Clive waited to make sure Holly was going deeper into the woods before he headed on foot to the wreckage. The flames were still soaring high, but the tail section had almost burnt out by now. Debris lay scattered on the ground, some of it smoking. As he drew closer, the heat made him take a step back.

He continued to look around to make sure no one was approaching, and when satisfied, he went back to look at the plane. He had never seen it before. From time to time there was a local crop duster who would spray farms and crops, but this was not it. A small packet smoldered just a few feet away from him and he walked over to it. Drugs like the ones he had seen at the Mitchells' house. He rolled it over with his foot to be certain. Yep. It looked like the same kind of fentanyl. That didn't mean this was the source of the Mitchells' drug involvement, but it was a possibility. How long had this been going on? Considering the deep ruts left from the vehicles, it wasn't a new thing.

A sinking feeling hit his gut. Someone had been using Cantrell land to smuggle drugs. Deacon, their dad, had been a Texas Ranger. Clive had been a deputy sheriff and Hawk had been in investigations with the army. Cash was a state trooper, in hopes of becoming a Texas Ranger like their dad. Even Emma had joined the military. He did not believe anyone in his family could be involved in this.

But someone was. There were three people employed by the ranch. Owen, Sammy and Utah. Owen had been the ranch foreman for over ten years and his family had been a part of their family the entire time. Sammy had been on the ranch for over five years and had been nothing but an upfront employee. He was quiet and didn't talk much about his home life, but he seemed content and knowledgeable about animals in agriculture. Utah was the newest employee, having only been on the ranch for a year and a half. Hired just months before his dad had been killed.

He could not imagine any of the ranch employees being involved in this, but it could've been someone who was friends of the family.

The thought left Clive feeling empty and disappointed. Also, angry someone might try to take advantage of his family.

He didn't want to jump to conclusions until he knew something for certain. Several small pops from the fire continued and the sizzling showed no signs of slowing. He pulled out his cell phone and snapped a picture of the plane and then sent it to his brothers and sister. He knew there was no cell connection on this side of the ranch, but as soon as they came within range, hopefully, the text would send.

Next, he texted the sheriff to let him know what was going on and requested help. He looked back to the tree line and didn't see Holly. Good. That meant she was hidden and had taken his warning seriously.

He considered whether he should take her back to the shack and check it out now or simply wait and hide to see who showed up. Holly's safety took precedence even though he was tempted to stay here. He needed her to be safe, and then he could worry about who was behind the attacks.

He turned toward the trees and waved to let her know to come out. Three seconds later, she emerged from the trees on Duchess. Still no sign of Binion. Hopefully, he hadn't run back to the ranch.

Holly rode up to him and said, "Come on. You can ride with me."

He wouldn't have minded because the shack was still probably a mile away, but he wanted to make sure she was comfortable as possible and not stressed. He would walk fast and make good time. "I can walk."

The words were no more out of his mouth than an engine sounded from the west on the opposite side of the airstrip. They both looked at each other. He said, "Let's move."

She removed her foot from the stirrup, and he quickly climbed on behind her and they took off for the trees, barely making it before a red pickup truck came over the horizon. There were several people who drove one just like that, but he continued to get farther away and make sure they were hidden in the foliage. Whoever it was when they saw the flames and the smoke would've known what happened. They would be searching for whoever had brought them down. The pilot might have called whoever they were supposed to meet.

Duchess was a calm girl, but no one had ridden double on her in a few years. She tossed her head at the extra weight but did as she was directed and continued at a fast pace. He looked back at the truck, which was not slowing down at the wreckage.

In the distance, a fast-moving creature ran across the airstrip, and he recognized Binion. The horse had stayed in the area. No doubt, whoever was in the red truck had seen him, giving away that Clive was in the area.

The truck hurried past the plane and continued in their direction. Clive didn't think they had been spotted, but now he wasn't certain.

Holly leaned back against him and put her mouth to his ear. "They're coming right for us."

He pulled Duchess to a stop behind a big cedar. There were a lot of pine trees on the ranch, but the cedar trees were bulkier, which he was grateful for. He whispered, "Be still. I don't think we've been spotted yet."

She did as he asked but looked down at the horse, as if staring at the man would draw his attention. The red truck continued at a fast clip across the airstrip, and when it got to the end of the runway, brake lights came on. Then the truck turned around and began to drive along the perimeter. It was coming toward them, giving them less than twenty seconds. Clive was almost certain they were hidden well, but he wasn't willing to take the chance. He nudged Duchess with his boot to head deeper into the foliage. They had gone about ten feet when the truck approached. Again, Clive moved behind a cedar and stopped.

The truck slowed down. The window was down, and an elbow rested on the doorframe. Clive tried to get a good look at the man, but there were simply too many shadows in the cab of the vehicle.

The truck slowly eased by. Clive thought they had made it undetected, when the backup lights came on. He whispered, "He's coming back."

They both sat still as the red vehicle stopped twenty yards from where they sat. Clive could no longer see the man, but he heard a door open and shut. He reached in the back of his waistband and pulled out his gun again. The weapon held only fifteen rounds, and he had already shot half of those. He wasn't exactly certain of the number.

The last thing they needed was a shootout with Holly next to him. Was he never going to get away from the likeness this had to the situation with Giselle? This time if there was gunfire, Holly would not be at his side.

Carefully he slid off the back of the horse and landed with a soft thud. He glanced up at Holly's face and saw the fear. He gave her a nod and patted her knee to reassure her that he had this before weaving into the tree branches. He hoped Duchess remained quiet. Footsteps approached, and there was a blur of movement through the limbs. A maroon shirt. Clive was still near Holly and stepped to the left, trying to stay hidden.

When he'd gone several more feet with his gun ready, he called out loud and clear, "That's far enough. Drop your weapon."

He still couldn't see the man's face, but the footsteps had stopped. Clive leaned to the right and suddenly he could see the man's cowboy felt hat. He still couldn't see his face as he wore the hat low on his head. "Drop it."

The repeated command had the man thinking, but that

was a bad thing. Criminals always thought they were stronger and faster than the next guy.

Duchess stomped her foot, and the man's hand jerked. Clive fired.

There was fast movement through the brush, and then Clive took off chasing the guy.

He watched the blur move through the trees. When he came out into a small clearing, his gaze landed on the man. It was a skinny, young guy. Almost like Owen's son, Lane. He didn't see the kid often, but this man was similar to him. The guy shot from over his shoulder behind him. The bullet whizzed past Clive and hit somewhere in the trees. He slowed a tad to make sure, but he didn't want to lose this guy. The man fired two more times.

Clive stepped behind the trunk of a pecan tree and fired again. The man grabbed his thigh and stumbled forward to his truck.

"Stop."

Just as Clive went to fire again the man opened his truck door, shielding him from Clive's aim. The man slammed the door, and keeping low, started the truck and took off. Not wanting to use all of his ammunition, Clive's arm fell to his side. He tried to get a read on the license plate but couldn't make out the numbers. Using his cell phone, he snapped a few quick shots hoping that once it was enlarged, he could read it.

He hurried back through the trees and found Holly where he had left her. He was glad she had listened to him. Her face was pale. "You didn't get shot?"

He shook his head. "No, but our guy got away but not until after he took a bullet in the leg."

"Where do we go now? Back to the ranch?"

"No." He wanted to check out the shack to see if anyone had been staying there. "It'll be getting dark soon. Let's go to the shack. I don't know how many people are involved in what I am guessing is drug dealing, but you can bet there will be more people on the way. I don't want us to be caught out in the open."

He hoped they could make it to the shack without another attack, and that there would be no one waiting for them when they got there. Their lives depended on it.

FOURTEEN

Clive had been quiet ever since they had left the clearing and were headed to the shack. Even though she was still on Duchess and he was on foot, they would make good time. Night had fallen fast in the pine trees, and it wouldn't be long until they would not be able to see except under the moonlight.

Twice they had seen Clive's horse in the distance grazing and sometimes watching them. No doubt he was confused about what he should do. But a couple of times in the last few minutes, she had heard movement through the trees and Clive had said he thought it was Binion because horses will try to stay close to other horses.

"When we get there, I want you to stay in the trees while I check out the shack and make sure no one is inside."

"I understand, but I don't like sitting in the trees in the dark. I don't know what I would do if you went down."

He pointed at the ground in front of them. "You see that trail?"

"Yeah. Might be an animal trail."

He shook his head. "Not that one. Animal trails are usually narrower unless there are big herds moving through. Except for pigs, not much around here is going to trample the ground that much. That's made by man."

She swallowed hard. She didn't like it, but she would do what he asked her to because she realized the danger checking out the shack put them in. And they had to find out who was behind the attacks.

He held up his hand. "Stop right there. The shack is about thirty yards ahead of us in the trees. You need to get off of Duchess in case you have to flee. There are too many low hanging lambs, and I don't want you to get knocked off of the horse."

He offered his hand to her and assisted her off the horse. When her feet touched the ground, she took a step forward, bumping into him. "Sorry."

He stared down into her face, his eyes searching hers. "It's okay. I know this has been a long few days for you and you're bound to be exhausted. I promise this will be over soon."

She swallowed when he didn't move to put distance between them, so she did. "I'm hoping no one is at the shack."

"Me too. I'll come get you if it's clear." He turned and swiftly moved down the trail. She could no longer see him nor could she hear his steps. For a big man, he traveled quietly.

Please Lord, keep him safe.

He had surprised her when he had not moved back when she bumped into him. She didn't want to make too big a deal out of that, but her instincts told her that maybe he didn't mind so much. It wouldn't matter if he was interested in her. Not that she believed he was. She had already told herself she would never get involved with someone again until she was on solid ground on her own. She would not need someone. That's what happened when Alec had stepped into her life. She had gone from living with her cruel aunt to being on her own. Yes, she had been making it, barely. So when Alec came along and paid her attention she had fallen fast.

And it was a relief that he had money and the burden of providing for herself was no longer hers. A couple of birds played in the tree limbs above her, and something skittered across the ground in a blur. Her heart beat a little faster even though she knew the animal was much too small to be a man. A squirrel jumped to the forest floor, bounced across the leaves and jumped back into a tree. Her hand went to her chest in relief.

Duchess stomped her foot on the ground. Holly ran a hand across her mane and patted her neck. She whispered, "I know you're tired, girl."

Holly glanced back in the direction that Clive had gone. He should be inside by now. She prayed he was safe. A dim yellow glow came through the trees, making her wonder if he'd made it inside. As the seconds slowly ticked by, she became more anxious.

Suddenly she thought she heard movement, and she stilled. She listened but didn't hear it again. Maybe it was his horse coming through the woods.

She stepped closer to Duchess. Suddenly, Clive stepped out of the trees. "You can come on in with me now."

Her hand went to her chest. "You scared me half to death. You walk awfully quiet through the woods for a big guy." When he didn't respond, she knew something had to be wrong. "Was everything okay?"

"The shack has been used for storing drugs. I wish I knew how long this has been going on. It makes me wonder if my dad had learned something that he shouldn't have. Is it possible this had to do with his death?"

Holly didn't blame him for asking himself those questions, but he would have to have proof and when he had explained how he found his dad it sounded like an accident to her also. "Did you find something at the shack that shows your dad was there?"

"Not yet." He waved her to come on as they entered the small front porch to the shack. Now seeing it, she wondered if she would've ever been able to find the place on her own because it was well hidden in the trees. She followed him inside and was assaulted by a musty and dusty odor. She supposed it was from being in the woods that gave it this smell. Moss had grown on the ground in many areas she had noticed.

It was one small room of about sixteen by twenty feet. Three oils lamps hung on different walls to light up the shack, the tiny flames barely flickering. A small stove stood in the corner, and old wooden bunk beds stood against the wall. There were several mismatched chairs stacked about. All of this was what she had envisioned, but what did surprise her were the boxes stacked along one wall. There were probably thirty of them that took up half of the floor space.

She nodded toward the boxes. "All of these are drugs?"

"I haven't had time to look in them except the first two boxes. It stands to reason since those two contained drugs, the rest will also. I don't know if the incoming plane was here to pick up drugs or to drop them off."

"Maybe the SIM card will tell us who's been involved."

Concern crossed his features. "I think you're right."

"What do we do now? The sheriff needs to be here." She had no desire to go traipsing back through the woods at night, but she also didn't want to stay in the shack with the drugs.

He rubbed his chin as he looked around at the boxes. "I don't like sitting here. It makes me think of campers who leave their food in the open when bears are known to be in the area. Just a matter of time before the animal will take you up on your offer."

"So... Are you saying we wait for them, or we leave?" Frankly, Holly was tired. Tired physically, and tired of thinking about the men who wanted to harm them.

The sun had set, and except for the light of the lamps, the shack was dark. She could barely make out Clive's eyes in the blackness.

"We need to find cell reception. The sheriff needs to be alerted to what is going on. It's possible someone else saw the smoke from the plane or heard the explosions and will call it in to authorities."

"I'm ready to go if it will help find the person who was supposed to meet the pilot." Even though they weren't certain, the logical conclusion was the Mitchells were tied to the drugs at their home and the ones the Cessna had planned to deliver or pick up. Had they crossed the dealers?

"Follow me." Clive blew out the lamps and headed out the door with her on his heels. "Binion, old man, glad to see you came back."

Sure enough, Clive's horse was standing beside Duchess. His head tossed in the air as his owner approached. The cowboy grabbed both sets of reins and started back up the trail. "We'll mount when we make out of the dense woods."

Her feet ached and were tender. When she'd purchased the cheap tennis shoes at the store, she hadn't planned on traipsing across the countryside. A blister was forming on the back of her right foot.

She was able to follow more from the sound of Clive and the horses than by sight. Suddenly, he stopped, and she almost ran into the back of Duchess. "What is it?"

He sliced his hand through the air, telling her to be quiet.

She couldn't see or hear anything, but she was certain his sudden warning couldn't be good.

Clive held still as he listened. He had thought he heard someone coming up the trail. He motioned for Holly to follow to the left, and away from the airstrip. He led the horses into the brush, but he was afraid they were making too much noise not to be heard.

When they had gone about twenty yards into the dense brush, he pulled Holly close. He whispered in her ear, "Stay right here, and I will be right back."

He was glad she didn't argue, but he quickly moved the horses into the deeper brush and then tied the reins securely to a thick limb. Then he hurried back, moving silently to Holly's side. "Have you seen anyone?"

She turned her face toward him, putting them only about an inch apart. So close he could feel her warm breath on his cheek. "No one."

For a fraction of a second, they simply stared into each other's eyes, and then he looked back at the trail. She was becoming more important to him, more so than just a person he was trying to keep alive. That scared him more than anything. At one time, he had cared a lot and even loved Giselle when she was shot. He did not know if he could go through that again, but if he did, he was certain it would be with someone like Holly. That meant it was more important than ever to catch these guys and ensure her safety.

Footsteps came up the trail. They both sank lower as the person got closer to the shack.

Whoever it was, he seemed to be taking his time and was cautious. They waited for what seemed forever, so the guy must've been farther away than what Clive had first believed. Maybe they had escaped being detected by the person.

Suddenly a flashlight turned on and pointed in the direction of the shack.

Clive wondered even though he had turned out the lamps, if the smell of the oil burning still lingered in the air. He hoped to get an identity on the man without having to put his and Holly's lives in the line of fire. Being that it was dark, and they were deep in the woods, he didn't figure the other person could see them well, nor could Clive see to shoot back. A dim light shone in one of the windows and a shadow went by. He couldn't tell if it was the man who had raced across the runway in his truck or not.

He didn't know how long they would have to wait for the man to return outside, but a couple of seconds later the man appeared in the doorway and glanced around.

One of the horses whinnied.

Suddenly the man disappeared inside, and his flashlight went out.

The man must've heard the horse. Boots clicked on the rickety wooden porch and a shadow crossed the trail. Clive waited until the sounds evaporated into the night before he turned to Holly. "I'm getting the horses."

He hurried back into the brush and then hightailed it back to Holly. He didn't want to have a shootout with a pregnant woman at his side, but he also didn't want to lose this guy. They continued hiking until they were at the edge of the densest part of the woods. Then he whispered, "I want you to stay right here. I'm taking Binion and going after this guy, but I want you to stay out of sight. Like I said earlier, if something happens to me, and I don't return, I want you to hightail it back to the ranch. Call the sheriff and Hawk as soon as you get a signal. Do you understand?"

"Oh, Clive, no. I won't leave you."

"I'll be back. But I need you to stay safe, and if I worry about you following me or not listening, it will distract me. Don't do it."

"That's not fair." She stared at him for a couple of seconds.

"The guy is getting away. Stay here. If you hear gunshots, I'll be back within five minutes. If not, take this trail to the east and go. Promise me."

"I promise." She stood on her tiptoes and gave him a peck on his cheek. "Stay safe."

He wrapped an arm around her waist, drawing her against his chest. He gave a sound kiss on her lips. "Gotta go."

He put his hands under her arms and gently put her on Duchess. Without saying another word, he stepped into the saddle and took off up the trail, trying to make up time. He should make-up ground quickly as he was on a horse, but he still had to stay watchful that the man wasn't waiting on him.

Clive clenched the reins in his fist as he knew it was only a matter of time. If the attacks kept coming, he or Holly would be seriously injured. He didn't like leaving her in the woods, but it was his best option. He topped a small rise and slowed. A bulky stand of brush sat along the trail on the right. Instead of going down the middle of the path, he swung right. If a man waited on him like he thought, he wanted to do the unexpected.

He slid his Glock 22 from its holster and held it ready as he approached the bush.

Something flashed from the trees to the west a fraction of a second before pain exploded in his shoulder. A man ran out of the brush straight toward him.

There were two men!

Clive fired at the gunman who came from the brush and then spun his horse around toward the trees. He couldn't see his target, but he fired two rounds before kicking his heels in Binion's sides and took off.

More gunfire came from behind him. He thought he'd made it as Binion galloped up the trail, but then a bullet struck his saddle horn. His horse shook his head and stepped down into a shallow ravine. Binion lost his footing and fell to the dirt, smashing Clive's thigh against the ravine's wall, before jumping back to his feet. Clive tried to hang on, but the saddle slipped sideways.

Clive lost his grip and fell, rolling three times before coming to a stop. Binion took off and disappeared into the night along with Clive's Winchester rifle that was still in the scabbard. No doubt the men had seen him go down. He didn't know if he'd hit the man who had emerged from the brush or not, but the man in the trees was still out there.

He prayed Holly would not wait around but get back to the ranch before the man went looking for her.

FIFTEEN

Holly heard the gunshots and had yet to cease praying that Clive was all right. She waited exactly where he'd told her to, but with each second that ticked by, she became more anxious. She needed to flee.

He'd told her if he wasn't back in five minutes... But if the man in the truck or the one at the shack—if it wasn't the same man—had known she was with Clive, wouldn't he come looking for her immediately? She believed he would. She nudged Duchess east, toward the ranch. She went only about thirty yards and stopped to listen for Clive approaching. He would be riding Binion if everything went as planned. She listened but only heard the wind blowing.

Duchess stomped her foot impatiently.

"Hold on, girl. We need to do what Clive said." She glanced at her cell phone and noted it had only been two minutes since she heard gunfire, but it seemed like forever.

Suddenly, a voice carried on the wind. Clive wouldn't be talking to anyone. If he was talking with someone, he'd holler to let her know it was him.

This had danger written all over it.

She again nudged the palomino. A long hill showed in

front of them, and they hit it at a run. When she got to the top, she glanced back at the place she was supposed to wait for Clive. Someone was there, but it wasn't Clive. She had grown familiar with the cowboy's confident swagger.

She led Duchess through the barbwire gate and they took off again. Soon, the trail disappeared, and she didn't know which way to get back to it. Right now, she had to get away. Surely, he hadn't been shot. The thought made her stomach swirl. Clive had been adamant she return to the ranch. As soon as she got reception, she'd call the sheriff and Hawk just like he'd said.

Someone hollered, but it wasn't Clive's voice. She didn't slow.

A gunshot rang out. She had no idea how close the bullet was, but she kept going. Once she made it to the next hill, she continued at a quick pace. She dodged trees and bushes.

It was a half-moon tonight, but as clouds drifted, her view was blurred. She tried to find the North Star so she could keep it on her left and ride due east, but it was simply too cloudy to make out the stars. If the man was able to use the red truck that had been on the runway, he could beat her back to the ranch. Not knowing what had happened to Clive or the man, she needed to be extra careful.

She continued to ride straight, using the moon as a guide. Normally, she wasn't directionally challenged, but she wasn't certain the moon was to the southeast like she thought. Right now, it was more of a gut feeling that she was riding in a straight line the way she and Clive had come.

Scenarios of what might have happened to Clive plagued her mind, but she fought the temptation to dwell on them. He'd told her to return to the ranch and that's what she would do. Then there was the kiss. She had never been so bold in her life to kiss a man without an invitation, but it had seemed right. Then he kissed her back. Her lips still tingled.

All she knew was that she trusted him.

Thirty minutes went by and then an hour. She thought she would have ridden past something that looked familiar, but it was just pastures, dotted with trees and sometimes dense woods. Everything looked alike. Occasionally, she passed cows bedded down in the grass.

After another hour, fear crept up on her that she was lost. Was she even on the Thunder Ridge Ranch? She assumed since she hadn't crossed any fences except for the gate she'd gone through, that she was. She checked her cell phone again for reception, but there was nothing. If she kept going, she had to come upon a road or something. Because of the darkness, she kept Duchess at a walk.

Sometime later, she topped the hill to see a structure amid the trees. There was at least one, but she couldn't tell if it was a house or a shop of some kind. While keeping a lookout for the man and the red truck, she slowly rode closer while sticking to the coverage of the trees.

As she drew near, she realized the building was a small frame home. No lights were on, but considering it was late, that didn't surprise her. She couldn't tell if anyone lived there or not.

She reined Duchess to a stop just outside the small yard and watched it for a minute. Nothing moved. If there was a dog, Holly hadn't alerted it yet.

Ride to the ranch. Clive's words came back to her. He'd be looking for her there and might even be there already, wondering where she was. But she never found the trail again and didn't know how far she was from it. Who would live here? It had to be someone from the ranch.

A bad feeling came over her. She needed to leave. If someone else lived on the ranch, wouldn't Clive or Shaylee have mentioned it? She hadn't crossed any roads, so she must still be on Thunder Ridge Ranch.

Suddenly, a voice came from behind her. "You look lost."

She turned in the saddle.

Owen stood at the edge of the trees. He stepped toward her. "Why don't you come on down, and I'll give you a ride to the ranch?"

It wasn't what he said as much as it was how he said it. There was no friendliness in the tone. "No," she carefully said, and prepared to bolt. "I'm supposed to meet Clive."

"You're a mile from the ranch. I have a landline if you want to come in and use the phone."

She was only a mile away but didn't know how to get there, especially in the dark. She needed to call the sheriff and Hawk. Clive had given her the knife to protect herself. "Okay, I appreciate it."

He smiled.

Hurriedly, she fished the knife from the saddle bag and held it with her right hand. Owen held a hand up to her to help her down from the left side of the horse. His palm felt clammy, and the bad feeling grew worse.

She would make the phone calls and then leave. It made her feel bad for not quite trusting the foreman, but there was too much at stake to take chances. Careful to keep the knife under the tail of her flannel shirt, she tied Duchess's reins to a bush, but it was difficult while keeping the weapon hidden. She followed Owen up the wooden steps of the porch and inside the home. After she stepped into the dark room, she waited for him to turn on a light.

"I'm sorry you've had so much trouble since you came to Cedar Hollow. You seem like a nice lady." Owen turned on a flashlight.

Was he the one at the line shack with the flashlight? The first thing she noticed was the broken furniture stacked in the corner and then trash on the floor. No one lived here, and it appeared no one had in a long time. She flipped up a light switch, but it remained dark.

"The electricity is off, darlin'." The glow of his teeth in the dim light showed an ugly smile.

No utilities meant no working phone lines either. He'd tricked her. She had no intention of sticking around to discuss things and headed for the door. She moved to go around him.

"I can't let you leave." He stepped in her way and grabbed her wrist. "You've seen too much. Sometimes people have the worst luck. You shouldn't have been there when Tim and Sabrina went down."

She pointed the knife at him. "Let go."

"Put that thing away." He didn't release his grip.

She'd never be able to overpower the foreman, but she was determined not to go down without a fight. Clive needed to know Owen was behind this. She tightened her grip on the handle. She didn't want to stab him, but she would if forced to.

Anger crossed his features. "Don't be more trouble than you're worth. I should have gotten rid of you a long time ago."

She was trapped, and she was not about to go down because of this evil man. Her very life and the life of her baby depended on her making a good decision. She did not want to kill him, but she did not want to give him another chance at murder. "Get back."

He took a step to the side, but didn't give her much room.

"More. Get away from the door," she commanded. Her heart raced wildly.

He laughed and shook his head. "You can't hit me."

Quickly, before she had time to change her mind, she reared back, and threw it.

The blade hit his thigh and bounced off, hitting the base of a lamp that was sitting on the floor and caused it to explode. Owen jumped at the sound and hit a coffee table, making him fall.

Holly did not wait around for him to react but took off out the back door as fast as she could move. She hurried into the woods. The back door slammed open behind her, and she kept moving as fast as she could, keeping her hand under her belly for support. She ran behind a tree and then began to circle back around to the front yard to the horse. But when she got there, she saw Owen's Jeep, which he'd driven on the ranch. For just a moment, she stood still, hoping the foreman would go in the other direction. When she heard him move past and deeper into the woods, she hurried toward his vehicle.

Duchess was munching grass and was no longer tied up. The horse looked up at her as she made it to the truck and flung the door open. She jumped in and looked for the keys but did not see them. "Oh no. Oh no. Where are they?"

He must have taken them with him. She scrambled out and made for the horse when he stepped out of the trees with his gun raised. "That's far enough." He took a couple of steps toward her with his gun still aimed. "I didn't want it to come to this. But there was no way for us to know you would be at the Mitchell house. You should've never involved Clive. You leave me no choice."

Holly swallowed hard. She wanted to get on the horse and ride away but there was no escape. He would shoot her if she tried. "You always have a choice. Let me go. It was not you who killed Tim and Sabrina." She took another step toward the horse.

"I have a family, and I'm not going to give up my life to go to prison for you."

The horse's reins were on the ground, and Holly only needed two more steps to be able to reach them. She moved a little closer. "It's too far gone, Owen. Even if you kill me right now, the sheriff is still searching for you. They are close to Clive."

He chuckled. "I have people on the inside of the sheriff's department. Clive won't be able to help you now. If he's still alive, he won't be for long. Then there will be no more witnesses. I hate to do it for he's a good guy, although naïve."

Her heart constricted. Was Clive really dead? *Please, Lord, let that not be so.*

Careful to keep his head down, Clive crawled up the side of the embankment and glanced over. He didn't see any movement. Someone hollered a few minutes ago, and he hoped Holly had not been spotted. She should be riding for the ranch. His leg throbbed from where Binion fell on him—the same leg that had taken a bullet years earlier—but once he was on his feet, he shoved the pain to the back of his mind. He needed to move fast.

Staying low, he ran along the edge of the ravine back to the where the man had fallen. It took Clive several minutes picking his way the safest way possible. A body lay face down on the ground.

He knelt beside it and rolled him over. It was the older hit man, and the badge was still attached to his waistband. Clive pulled it off and read it. It said CC Police Department, and stood for Corpus Christi, the same place the younger hit man, Brodie Hoffman, was from.

Where did the other man go? He glanced around but didn't see him. How had both gotten back here? From what he could see, there had only been one man in the red truck. This one must have either ridden with him or had another mode of transportation. Clive wanted to get to Holly as quickly as possible. The truck might be close.

Remaining hidden as much as possible, he jogged in the direction the other shooter had been lying in wait. He kept his Glock in his hand.

Suddenly, headlights shone through the trees. He stepped behind a pine and waited for the vehicle to approach. When it came out of the brush, he realized it was same red truck he'd seen earlier. It headed down the trail toward the body. When it was only twenty yards away and was even with Clive, he stepped out from the tree. "Stop."

Brake lights flashed. Instead of stopping, the driver floored it and swung the truck around at Clive.

Clive fired twice. The windshield shattered and the truck veered to the left before rolling to a stop. With his gun still aimed, he hurried to the driver's side. "Get out of the truck."

The driver slumped forward.

Clive swung the door open. The young man was bleeding and had pressed a hand to his neck. He recognized the kid. "Lane?"

"Don't shoot me again."

Clive had no intention of shooting Owen's son, but he also knew the kid was carrying a gun and had shot at him. He quickly leaned into the cab of the truck, grabbed the pistol that lay on the seat and tossed it into the bed of the truck. "Scoot over. I'll get you help just as soon as you tell me what's going on."

Lane writhed in pain. "I can't move. I'm dying."

"You're not dying." No doubt he was in pain, but Clive had little sympathy for anyone who would shoot another man from the back. "Move over and get to talking."

To help him, Clive leaned his shoulder into the kid and shoved him across the seat into the passenger side. Lane cried out, and Clive climbed into the driver's seat. He threw the truck into gear and took off across the land. He knew there was no way he could cross the way he and Holly had ridden, so he said, "Which way? I'll get you to a hospital as soon as I can. How do I get out of here?"

"That way." He pointed toward the airstrip. The kid groaned and now clutched both his neck and shoulder. Clive knew Lane was in pain and probably was telling him the truth. On the other side of the airstrip, there was a narrow path that led back through the trees. A narrow, but newer wooden bridge crossed the creek and led out to the other side. "Did your daddy build this bridge?"

"Just get me to the hospital."

Clive hit the brakes. "You're in no position to argue. If you want the bleeding to stop, you need to tell me what's going on."

"Dad had it built. Me and Jake did most of the work. Don't let me bleed to death."

The bleeding had almost stopped. He thought the bullet had hit more on the shoulder than on the neck, but it'd make him talk more if he believed it was worse than it was. After about half a mile, the road ended at a corner fence post. Clive and the rest of the brothers would have little reason to come back here or notice the barbwire gate at this part of the property.

"Call an ambulance."

"We don't get cell reception."

"You do over this hill at the old Baxter place. That's what my dad called it. That's where we always go to use our cell phones."

Baxter was the name of the family that owned the land before his dad bought the place. The house had sat empty for years before then. He couldn't believe the ranch foreman who had worked for the Cantrells for ten years had betrayed them. Right now, Clive needed to call the sheriff and make certain Holly had made it back to the ranch.

He turned to Lane. "Where is your dad now?"

"I don't know. He said he had something to take care of."

He didn't like the sound of that. As he neared the old Baxter home, he stopped and checked his cell phone. There was one bar. He quickly called the sheriff and let him know what he was doing. As he neared the house, the first thing he noticed when his headlights hit the yard was a horse in the front yard. From this distance, he couldn't tell if it was Duchess or Binion. As he pulled up, his heart sank as he realized it was Duchess.

Holly was here. He prayed she was safe and hadn't ran into Owen.

"Stay here." He slammed the gear into Park.

"Don't forget to call—"

Clive had already slammed the door on Lane's words. He didn't see the Jeep that Owen normally drove. But in his gut, he knew Holly and Owen had been here. With his gun ready, he hurried inside to see if anyone was there. A lamp was smashed in the corner and a bullet casing rested on the old carpet.

He strode back out and got in his truck.

"Did you call for help?"

Clive ignored the kid and drove around the north side of the house looking for Holly. He raced up the hill with dirt flying in his rearview mirror from his tires, and when he topped out on the horizon, he saw Owen's Jeep at the bottom of the valley.

He slowed down, not wanting to rush upon them and not knowing what was going on. In Clive's haste, he did not want Owen to panic and shoot Holly.

He eased his truck behind the trees. He needed to make it as far down the hill as he could before being spotted.

"That's my dad's Jeep."

"Stay here." He climbed out and was careful not to slam the door. Lane might try to get Owen's attention, but he didn't care at the moment. He needed to find Holly. Moving swiftly and quietly, he weaved between the trees and moved down the hill. There was rustling somewhere below him and to his left. Then there was more movement. He stopped to listen. Footsteps. He pushed deeper into the ticket, careful of each step and kept his gun ready.

"You might as well give up." It was Owen's voice. "You're only dragging out the inevitable."

The foreman must've been talking to Holly. He squinted to get a better look as the man came into view.

He still couldn't see Holly and was afraid to shoot until he knew her position. There was simply too much brush to be able to see his target and it was dark. A rustling to his right gained his attention. He continued to silently move forward.

"Hey!" Owen yelled.

Clive glanced up to see the foreman hurrying his way. Taking a chance, he quietly said, "Holly."

There was no answer, but Clive continued in the same direction. Then he saw her. She was in a small clearing, trying to walk uphill. Blood soaked her left sleeve.

A gunshot blasted. Clive ran to Holly just as something whizzed past them. He wrapped his arms around her, spinning her around to put himself between her and the gunman.

"I'm so glad you're here." She breathed. "Owen is the one who's been trying to kill me."

"I know. Shh." He held on to her as he propelled her through the trees.

"If I die and the baby survives, I want you to take care of the baby."

"You're going to be fine." He couldn't think about Holly not making it. "I will get you to safety."

Something hit him in the bicep and a fraction of second later, the blast sounded. The hit spun him around, and he fell to the ground.

"Clive!" Holly's hands clawed at his shirt.

He had to protect her. He wasn't going to let her down.

SIXTEEN

Holly leaned over Clive. Her heart raced when she saw him go down. None of this was supposed to ever happen. How had things gotten so out of control? She dropped beside him.

Clive struggled to his feet, his right arm dangling at his side. He held the gun in his left hand. "Stay down, Holly."

Steps sounded behind them. She turned, but didn't see anyone. She continued to look because she was certain she'd heard footsteps. A yelp sounded up the hill.

"I don't want to have to shoot, Owen," Clive called, "but don't doubt me, I will."

A laugh sounded from the trees. Staying on her knees, she crawled behind the protection of a tree trunk a couple of feet from Clive. Holly held her breath and waited for Owen to present himself.

A twig snapped behind her. A tall cowboy disappeared behind a pine tree on her left. She blinked, not certain who she'd just seen. A little farther up the hill, another man, this one a little stockier than the first, moved on the side of the trail. Even though she'd never met Clive's brothers, these two looked just like him.

Owen smiled, but there was no humor in it. "I should've taken you out a year ago, Clive."

"You mean just like you killed my dad."

The foreman's jaw twitched. "Deacon wouldn't listen to reason. He was determined to go to the authorities. He never was the smartest man."

Holly glanced at Clive and noticed the lack of expression on his face. She would've thought he would be furious, but all she saw was determination.

"You never stopped to consider what your drug involvement and murders were doing to you own son. Lane took one of my bullets. He's in the truck up the hill."

Owen eyes grew huge. He raised his gun. "I'll kill you."

"Put the gun down." The cowboy moved closer with his gun raised.

The stockier man held a weapon too. "Do what he says."

The foreman lowered the gun to his side.

To Holly's surprise another cowboy, this one a little younger and extremely handsome, came out from the brush directly behind her and Clive with a gun also pointed at the foreman. She felt like she was watching an old western movie.

"No!" Owen yelled as his gun hand jerked upward, but the sound of a single shot filled the air. Owen dropped to the ground holding his hand.

Sheriff Copeland's voice called across the open space. "Owen, you are under arrest for attempted murder of Holly Myers and Clive Cantrell." As the lawman trudged down the hill, he turned to Clive. "I'm glad your family came home."

Clive dropped his weapon to his side. "Me too. I was out of bullets, but I didn't want Owen to know that."

Holly's mouth dropped open. If his brothers and the

sheriff hadn't shown up when they did, Clive... Her mind couldn't go there.

"You can get up." Clive looked down at her. "You're safe now."

Deputy Jenkins hurried down the trail and read Owen his rights. While the deputy slapped handcuffs on the foreman, Holly turned to Clive. "You're hurt. We need to get you to the doctor."

The stockier man chuckled. "He'll live. It's not the first time Clive's been shot and probably won't be the last."

Clive rolled his eyes. "Holly, meet the annoying members of my family." He pointed to the stocky man. "This is Hawk." Then to the first cowboy on the scene. "Cash." Finally, he indicated the young handsome one. "And Sawyer."

She smiled. "I'm glad you all showed up when you did." She looked back to Clive. "Did you really shoot Owen's son?"

"I did, but he'll survive."

"Emma is keeping an eye on him at the moment," Cash said.

"The older hitman is dead, too," Clive added. "He was the one at the line shack. We'll learn his identity soon."

"Does that mean everyone is caught or dead? Like the danger is over?" Joy hoovered at the surface as she held her breath. After several days of fearing death, she was almost afraid to hope.

"It's over." For a long moment, his gaze held hers.

As the deputy walked up the hill with Owen in handcuffs and the brothers followed behind, Clive stared down at her with intense dark eyes. "Did Owen hurt you?"

Though Holly knew that Clive had to be in pain, his voice was so soft and caring, it almost undid her. Even with him shot and bleeding, his concern was for her. "I'm fine. I'm embarrassed to say I got lost on the way to the ranch. Owen was here. I shot at him but missed."

Sheriff Copeland made his way over and said, "Paramedics are on the way. Cantrell, you took another bullet this time. That's becoming a habit."

Clive glanced at him and half smiled. "At least this time she's okay."

Sheriff Copeland's seriousness returned. "Our investigators talked to Jake Griffin."

"Did you learn anything?"

"Seems like after someone tried to kill him, he believes it's safer to talk. He didn't see who shot him, but Jake admitted to helping Owen traffic drugs using the feed store. No one noticed a few truckloads being delivered occasionally. When we questioned him about you, he clammed up. And I questioned Jenkins after I saw you visiting him at the department. We're checking out Deputy Woods and any involvement he had with Tim Mitchell. Looks like Wood's not dealing but is a customer. We're still looking into it. We're going to have a lot of paperwork and man-hours on this, but that can wait until after you're tended to at the hospital. This young lady probably needs to be checked out also."

"Yes, sir."

Several minutes later, two more deputies had shown up about the same time ambulances sounded in the distance. Holly took a few steps back to distance herself from Clive. They had done it. They had both come out of this alive and had caught the killers. And now Clive could get back to his life and be assured that he could keep someone safe. That was what it was all about for him. Right?

Once the ambulances arrived, Holly walked around to

the far side to talk to a female paramedic who checked her vitals. Holly noted Clive glanced her way as he was helped onto a stretcher. Their eyes connected but she quickly turned in the other direction.

She sat in the back of the ambulance and purposely kept her back to Clive, trying to prepare herself for their relationship to be over. Her heart constricted at the thought, but she had been preparing for this moment for months. Ever since Alec had died, and she found herself alone facing the world. She needed to stand on her own. She would give her daughter a better life than what she had been given.

But even as the thoughts ran through her mind, she couldn't help but to be disappointed.

She wanted to be on her own. Didn't she?

Several minutes passed as the paramedic checked her out and asked Holly several questions. It was difficult to concentrate on what was being asked as she heard Clive talking to a paramedic on the other side of the ambulance. There was some mention of his thigh being injured when his horse fell on him.

The paramedic asked Holly to lay back so they could load her into the ambulance and get her to the hospital.

Before they shut the door, she heard Clive's voice. "Wait."

She drew a deep breath. She was surprised when he suddenly filled the open door. He pointed. "I want to talk to you after you are checked out at the hospital."

"There's no need. You did what you said you would do."

"Promise me you will not leave the hospital without talking to me."

"Clive, we both know…"

"Promise me."

She sighed. Just because he talked to her did not mean she had to do anything she did not want to. "I promise."

The paramedic stood beside Clive and said, "You need to get back on your stretcher before you pass out from the loss of blood. I'm certain that arm is going to require surgery."

Clive held his good hand in the air as if surrendering. "I will do as you say." Before he did as a paramedic directed, once again his gaze connected with hers as if he was going to ensure she kept her word.

Several hours later when Holly awakened, it took her a moment to realize where she was. Then everything slammed back into her when she realized she was in a hospital room. All except for the dim light above her bed, the room was dark, and a shadow lurked in the corner. A small sliver of light shone from underneath the closed door. The large windows on the far wall showed no light, meaning it must be nighttime.

Beside her bed a voice said, "I was beginning to worry about you."

Her gaze instantly moved to Clive who was sitting in a chair beside her bed, and halfway behind her where she had not immediately seen him. She was surprised he was in her room instead of in his own hospital room. "What are you doing here? Did they not have to perform surgery?"

He gingerly moved his chair closer to her where he could see her face better. A slow grin appeared on his lips. "It was a short procedure. They tried to keep me in my room. I'm afraid I'm not a very good patient."

She shook her head. "You need to take care of yourself, Clive. You don't need to protect me any longer. Unless something has changed, Owen was arrested and both of the Mitchells' killers are dead. Jake is still in hospital. I should be safe now." He reached across the bed and took her hand into his. She couldn't help but notice he cringed as if the movement caused pain. She wanted to tell him to be careful and that there was no need for him to be with her, but she knew he wouldn't take the suggestion. Clive was a stubborn cowboy who did not like being told what to do.

His smile faded into a serious expression. "I don't want you out of my life, Holly. I know I told you I felt the need to protect you, and that much was true. It's more than that. I've fallen in love with you."

"In love with me?" She shook her head. "I'm sure it was just in the heat of the moment. A time when your family was gone and the safety of a stranger landed squarely on your shoulders. In a few days, or even weeks, you will be ready to have your life back."

"You don't get it, do you?" He kissed her hand that he still held. "I want to spend time with you. It's not that difficult to understand. You don't have to do everything alone. I want to be there for you. And for the baby. If you don't like my company, tell me to go away and I will. But I wish you wouldn't."

Her hand still tingled from where he kissed it, making her feel safe and secure. It sounded too good to be true. Could she trust him? Alec had told her he cared for her, but it had all been a ruse.

He chuckled again. "I told you I want to spend my life with you. It's not a death sentence."

She smiled. This time he said he wanted to spend *his life* with her. "What are you asking?"

"When I first saw you trying to escape from those men, I wanted to protect you, mainly because I can't not help someone in need. But over the past few days, no matter how much I tried to resist, I've fallen for you. I prayed to God that I could find someone to complete me, but I didn't think it would happen until you came into my life. I want you to become my wife. I want to give you the family and home you deserve."

She'd come to Cedar Hollow to start a new life and had prayed to God she could provide a safe place to raise her child. No doubt, she was a different person than when she first arrived. Could she have fallen in love with the cowboy that fast? She took in his dark, hopeful eyes and her heart did a little flip. Yes, she believed she had. "Yes, Clive, I will happily marry you."

He pulled her into his arms and kissed her.

EPILOGUE

Clive held open the door as Holly walked through carrying baby Jeanine with her. He put the carrier on the floor and moved the blanket out of the recliner to make room for Holly.

She laughed. "I'm not helpless."

"I never said you were, but let a man feel useful." He shot her a smile.

She sat, and Clive moved the diaper bag next to her chair. He asked, "Do you need anything?"

"I have everything I need." And she meant that. They had gotten quietly married two weeks ago, with only his family and Shaylee in attendance. Rowan, Holly's brother, had not been able to make the trip from South Carolina, but he'd sent a Congratulations card with a gift card inside. Considering they hadn't talked in over two years, she found the gesture promising. Shaylee had insisted on moving back into the main house to let Holly and Clive have the cabin. Clive agreed, but only for the time it took to build their new cabin where the Baxter house stood. It was a compromise of being close to the ranch and the back of the property which Holly had thought was so secluded and beautiful.

She would've loved to have had a big wedding, but

more importantly, was ready to start her life with Clive. Big decorations did not seem that important compared to bringing little Jeanine home to a well-established family. She had redecorated the nursery with horses and daisies. Clive was adamant about not leaving out the old decorations Giselle had started. He claimed he wanted Holly to know Jeanine was not simply a replacement for his loss. He told her to feel free to create the room just for little Jeanine.

Margot came by the hospital after Holly gave her permission to have a short visit. The woman broke down in tears when Holly allowed her to hold the baby. Instead of fearing Alec's mom, now Margot looked like an aging, lonely person. Holly didn't trust the woman totally, but she also didn't want to sever ties with Jeanine's grandmother. She would probably never allow the woman to play a big part in her daughter's life, but she planned to take it one day at a time. With Clive and the Cantrell clan at her side, Margot didn't present the threat she once had.

After Owen's arrest, they learned Deacon had come upon the airstrip and tire ruts while searching for a lost cow and calf. He wanted to know who'd been using the airstrip and put out three deer cameras. To Clive's estimation, the day his father had been short with him was the day his dad confronted Owen. The foreman stabbed Clive's father and then staged the death to look like an accident on the tractor. Owen only found two of the cameras, but the SIM card of the third placed Owen at the scene. The man adamantly denied being the person who threw Holly out of the window or attacked her in the hospital. He blamed Jake Griffin for those incidents, and claimed Jake paid Derek Patel to shoot Clive and that Derek had unfortunately hit Giselle also.

Jake admitted to having an affair with Giselle, and authorities were investigating him for his part in the drug distribution and the attacks on Holly. The sheriff was also looking for a money trail to see if there was a connection between Jake and Derek Patel to prove Owen's claim that Jake was behind the shooting.

"Let me know when you're ready for Mom to come and visit. I told her I would text her to let her know. She promises she will not intrude but would love to come see the baby again."

Holly smiled. "She is welcome to come anytime. As is the rest of the family."

"Are you certain? I don't want you to overdo it. My family can be…"

She laughed. "Please, Clive, invite them up."

Thirty minutes later, they were surrounded by all the Cantrells. Nora held little baby Jeanine with a satisfied smile. "I wish your father were here," she said to Clive. "He would love this little girl."

Clive smiled. "I know he would have, Mom." The rest of the brothers and Emma were in the kitchen quietly talking. Holly sat on the couch so Nora could have the rocker with the baby. She didn't mind. Clive sat beside her and put his arm on the back of the cushion. She had never seen the cowboy act so content, even if he had been a little nervous at the hospital when she delivered her precious daughter. She had never figured the tough cowboy could be so sensitive and caring.

He looked at her now and whispered so only she could hear, "You're a great mom. You make me the happiest man in the world."

She leaned into his arm and laid her head on his shoulder. Laughter burst from the kitchen followed by someone shushing them.

Nora glanced up and shook her head. She mouthed, *Sorry. We're a loud bunch.*

Yes, they were loud and absolutely wonderful. Holly had never been so thankful to be part of a loving family and hadn't had the feeling of belonging until now. She thought Grandma Harvey and her dad would also be happy for the way things turned out for her.

Clive looked at her curiously. "What are you smiling about?"

"That I had moved to Cedar Hollow hoping for a quiet and safe life. I think rambunctious and safe is even better."

* * * * *

If you liked this story from Connie Queen, check out her previous Love Inspired Suspense books:

Justice Undercover
Texas Christmas Revenge
Canyon Survival
Abduction Cold Case
Tracking the Tiny Target
Rescuing the Stolen Child
Wilderness Witness Survival
Searching for Justice

Available now from Love Inspired Suspense!
Find more great reads at LoveInspired.com.

Dear Reader,

Thank you for joining me on Clive and Holly's journey. Holly wants to start a new life and get away from her problems, but she walks into trouble when she arrives in the unfamiliar town. Clive steps in to protect her, even though he is dealing with unresolved issues of his own. Both struggle to trust and must learn how to lean on others.

What about you? How do you tackle trust issues? Do you turn to God or try to handle everything on your own?

Shielded by the Cowboy is the first book of the Thunder Ridge Justice Series. Coming from a large, close-knit family of my own, I love stories about families, and I'm currently working on the next book in the series.

I love to hear from readers. You can connect with me on my Facebook page at www.facebook.com/queenofheartthrobbingsuspense, or keep up with my latest news and books on my website at www.conniequeenauthor.com.

Connie Queen

Get up to 4 Free Books!

We'll send you 2 free books from each series you try PLUS a free Mystery Gift.

FREE Value Over $25

Both the **Love Inspired**® and **Love Inspired**® **Suspense** series feature compelling novels filled with inspirational romance, faith, forgiveness and hope.

YES! Please send me 2 FREE novels from the Love Inspired or Love Inspired Suspense series and my FREE gift (gift is worth about $10 retail). After receiving them, if I don't wish to receive any more books, I can return the shipping statement marked "cancel." If I don't cancel, I will receive 6 brand-new Love Inspired Larger-Print books or Love Inspired Suspense Larger-Print books every month and be billed just $7.19 each in the U.S. or $7.99 each in Canada. That is a savings of 20% off the cover price. It's quite a bargain! Shipping and handling is just 50¢ per book in the U.S. and $1.25 per book in Canada.* I understand that accepting the 2 free books and gift places me under no obligation to buy anything. I can always return a shipment and cancel at any time by calling the number below. The free books and gift are mine to keep no matter what I decide.

Choose one:
- ☐ **Love Inspired Larger-Print** (122/322 BPA G36Y)
- ☐ **Love Inspired Suspense Larger-Print** (107/307 BPA G36Y)
- ☐ **Or Try Both!** (122/322 & 107/307 BPA G36Z)

Name (please print)

Address   Apt. #

City   State/Province   Zip/Postal Code

Email: Please check this box ☐ if you would like to receive newsletters and promotional emails from Harlequin Enterprises ULC and its affiliates. You can unsubscribe anytime.

Mail to the Harlequin Reader Service:
IN U.S.A.: P.O. Box 1341, Buffalo, NY 14240-8531
IN CANADA: P.O. Box 603, Fort Erie, Ontario L2A 5X3

Want to explore our other series or interested in ebooks? Visit www.ReaderService.com or call 1-800-873-8635.

---

*Terms and prices subject to change without notice. Prices do not include sales taxes, which will be charged (if applicable) based on your state or country of residence. Canadian residents will be charged applicable taxes. Offer not valid in Quebec. This offer is limited to one order per household. Books received may not be as shown. Not valid for current subscribers to the Love Inspired or Love Inspired Suspense series. All orders subject to approval. Credit or debit balances in a customer's account(s) may be offset by any other outstanding balance owed by or to the customer. Please allow 4 to 6 weeks for delivery. Offer available while quantities last.

Your Privacy—Your information is being collected by Harlequin Enterprises ULC, operating as Harlequin Reader Service. For a complete summary of the information we collect, how we use this information and to whom it is disclosed, please visit our privacy notice located at https://corporate.harlequin.com/privacy-notice. Notice to California Residents – Under California law, you have specific rights to control and access your data. For more information on these rights and how to exercise them, visit https://corporate.harlequin.com/california-privacy. For additional information for residents of other U.S. states that provide their residents with certain rights with respect to personal data, visit https://corporate.harlequin.com/other-state-residents-privacy-rights/.

LIRLIS25